FOREVER HER EARL

DUKES MOST WANTED
BOOK FOUR

SCARLETT SCOTT

Happily Ever After Books

Forever Her Earl

Dukes Most Wanted Book Four

For more information, contact author Scarlett Scott.

https://scarlettscottauthor.com

For my sister, with much love and thanks for always supporting my books

CHAPTER 1

*L*ucy Chartrand had possessed a great deal of good
fortune in her life, but at the moment, standing
beneath the black Yorkshire night and the dim glow
of a quarter moon, she was most concerned with her latest
bit of good luck: a footman named Robert. He was handsome
enough, young enough, and charming enough to have caught
her eye, and heaven knew she'd been casting her gaze far and
wide since she'd arrived at Sherborne Manor. Indeed, she'd
been looking for someone to aid her in her plan from the
moment she'd realized the little scandals she kept creating
weren't sufficient to deter dogged fortune hunters.

Yes, Robert would do. He would do quite well.

She waited for him in the gardens where they'd agreed to
meet after he had completed his duties for the evening, the
air warm around her and redolent with the scent of lush,
summer blossoms. A slight trill of nervousness went down
her spine, a skittish feeling she couldn't quite chase, regardless of her determination.

After tonight, everything would change. *She* would be
changed forever and, most importantly, free.

And she wanted it that way. Mother would have no choice but to accept that Lucy wanted a life of her own, a life that had nothing to do with marrying a proper English lord or anyone else, for that matter. She wanted a future that was hers to do with as she pleased. To start her cosmetics business as she'd dreamed. When she was no longer a prize on the marriage mart, Mother would have to concede.

The crunch of gravel alerted Lucy that she was no longer alone. He was coming to her. And although she felt a surge of excitement that her plan was finally coming to fruition, she could acknowledge that the thrill had far less to do with Robert than it did with her impending independence. Still, Robert was handsome and strapping. He admired her—she'd caught his stare more than once, and that was how it had begun.

The footsteps grew nearer, and she turned to find a decidedly masculine form moving toward her in the silvery glow of the fragmented moon. Was it her imagination, or did his shoulders seem broader, his height a bit taller than she had remembered? She didn't give herself a moment to fret over the concern, nonsensical that it was. Everyone looked different in the darkness, and he was here; he had come to her. If she hesitated at all, she would lose her courage.

Without a word, Lucy threw herself into his chest, entwining her arms around his neck. His hands settled on her waist, and he stumbled backward for a moment from either surprise or the force of her collision with him, she couldn't be certain. She decided it didn't matter as she rose on her toes and pressed her mouth to his.

She felt his sharply indrawn breath—perhaps she had shocked him with her boldness. It ceased to matter when he responded. His lips were fuller than she had recalled—in truth, she'd thought Robert's mouth a bit on the small side and not necessarily ideal for kissing. But she knew instantly

2

how wrong she'd been. Because at the mere contact of her mouth to his, a jolt went through her like an electrical current, warming her everywhere. Her body came to life, her senses acutely honed to almost painful awareness.

There was the hot, seductive glide of his lips over hers as he answered her kiss, the soft puff of his breath melding with hers, the decadent scent of him, and that was also new. Musk, the crisp freshness of citrus, a hint of pine. It ought to be a sin for a man to smell so divine. She inhaled, wanting more of it, more of him, growing bolder now. Her fingers slipped into his hair, which seemed a trifle longer than she had supposed, so soft and silken. The air around them felt as if it were shimmering with delicious, dangerous possibility.

She forgot to be nervous and followed her instincts. This illicit tryst was far better than she had believed it would be already, and relief mingled with desire, her spirits buoyed by the undeniable pull between herself and this man. He deepened the kiss, his lips guiding hers open, his tongue gliding into her mouth, and the kiss turned into something else.

Something sinful and wickedly delicious.

She made a sound of helpless yearning, clinging to his strong form, pressing herself against him, needing contact. Everywhere her curves melted into his hardness, she felt as if she were aflame.

Lucy had chosen her *toilette* with care this evening before she'd slipped from her guest chamber. She was wearing a simple bodice and skirt with only one petticoat for modesty and no corset. She was grateful for her lack of layers now as she rubbed her breasts against his chest, her nipples beaded and aching, her body guiding her down this dangerous path from which there would be no return. She wanted his touch there, she realized, where it was wrong for any man to touch a woman who wasn't his wife. She wanted it desperately.

"Touch me," she murmured against his mouth. "Please."

One of his hands slid from her waist, higher, higher, a slow and torturous movement that had her almost panting by the time he reached her breast, cupping it, his clever thumb stroking over her nipple.

He kissed her again, taking her mouth with a raw ferocity that made her knees go weak. Losing her virginity wouldn't be so terrible, Lucy thought wildly. Not with this man, not in the magic of this charmed night. There had been a moment earlier, when she had been preparing herself, when indecision had threatened to overwhelm her. She had questioned the wisdom of her plan. For half an hour, she'd convinced herself she should find a different means of thwarting Mother's plans. But now, she was glad she had come to the gardens tonight as intended.

Not just relieved, but overjoyed.

She kissed him with all the freshly awakened passion burning inside her, his tongue moving sinuously against hers, his other hand caressing from her waist to her bottom. He grabbed a handful of her rump and ground her lower body against his, and she could feel him, his hardness, the ridge rising to prominence in his trousers that meant he wanted her too.

Between her legs, she was throbbing and shamefully wet, her drawers already damp. She wondered what it would be like for him to touch her there, for him to lift her hems and run his big hands all over her. He squeezed her bottom, making a low, gruff sound of pleasure into her mouth. This was what she had been missing by being properly courted by stiff-backed suitors who salivated over her family's immense wealth. This was passion, pleasure, everything she longed for and read about in her books.

Everything she'd thought was fictional, forever beyond her reach.

And yet, here it was. Or rather, here *he* was, kissing her, holding her, touching her.

Lucy never wanted the night to end.

MISS LUCY CHARTRAND kissed like a courtesan.

Gareth Claremont, Earl of Rexingham, general stickler for propriety, knew he shouldn't be surprised at the discovery. Rather, he should be horrified. He should also stop kissing her, thrust her away from him as if she were fashioned of flame and he feared getting burned.

And he *would*, just as soon as he could summon his wits and restraint, both of which seemed to have fled him the moment she'd thrown herself into his arms and sealed her lips to his. Because something had happened in that fleeting, unexpected span of time in the moonlight. Something strange and unwanted. She'd barreled into him with a complete disregard for his lack of preparation, nearly sending him sprawling to his backside with her atop him.

But then, perhaps that had been her intention. There was no doubt about it, Miss Chartrand had ventured into the darkened gardens tonight to have an assignation. She wasn't wearing proper undergarments, a sinful but happy discovery according to his wayward cock. He shouldn't be allowing himself to wallow in such potent, all-consuming lust. It was dangerous, particularly given the female who was sighing so prettily into his kiss.

But her tongue was in his mouth and her fingers were sifting through his hair, and his hand possessed a will of its own, shaping one lovely breast, so soft and abundant, so deliciously full, and his thumb found her hard little nipple, grazing over it until she made a throaty sound, arching into him.

Not a courtesan, he decided. More like a witch, for surely she'd cast a spell upon him. He didn't even like the bold, brash American heiress whose lips were responding to his so deliciously. She was trouble, and he'd known it from the moment he'd first set eyes on her. Beautiful, maddening, tempting trouble. But trouble just the same.

He would stop kissing her soon. He'd summon up a stern admonishment, a reminder to them both of the perils of playing games with members of the opposite sex after midnight. He knew better.

Except now she had torn her mouth from his, and she was kissing along his jaw. Her hands, dainty hands he'd found himself admiring on more than one occasion over the course of the house party at which they were both guests, had slipped to his coat, pushing it over his shoulders. He shrugged it away, loving the way her caresses felt, despite himself. Her fingers were on his waistcoat, nimble and sure. Likely, this wasn't the first time she'd disrobed a lover.

Her lips were on his neck now, gliding like hot velvet, and he found himself desperate to return the favor. A handful of buttons bisected her thin, silk bodice. He left her breast with reluctance to slip one free from its mooring, telling himself he would stop at one. He merely wanted to know the satiny texture of her bare skin. He would stop then, put an end to this madness.

Her teeth scraped over his throat, and his cock twitched. His fingers found the second button, then the third. She fumbled with his neck cloth, tugging it free and flinging it somewhere. In the dim recesses of his mind, he knew this was a mistake. That he needed to extricate himself from her embrace and return to the haven of his bedchamber. To demand that she do the same.

He would.

Soon.

One more kiss.

Just another button.

But then another came free, and her bodice gaped open, and sweet merciful heavens, she wasn't even wearing a chemise beneath it. Little wonder her breast had felt so damned good in his hand, her nipple so ripe and hard. In the glow of the moonlight, her breasts were too tempting for him to resist. Beautiful and pale and ethereal, almost silver, and round and perfect, tipped with pink nipples that begged for his mouth.

He wasn't going to do it.

He wasn't going to...

Gareth's head dipped. He took the peak of her breast into his mouth, savoring the heat and softness of her, her ragged inhalation, the shape of the pert bud on his tongue. He suckled, lightly at first, but then with greater urgency when her fingers sank back into his hair and she raked her nails along his scalp with a breathy moan. She was so responsive, all soft and pliant against him, her leg hooking around his hip as if she couldn't get close enough to him. As if she sought to wrap herself around him, twine about him like a vine.

And he wanted her to.

He wanted nothing between them. No garments, no thought. He wanted her naked beneath him in a bed; he wanted all night to explore her. He wanted to sink his cock deep inside her and make her his.

But that was wrong.

He couldn't. She was an unmarried woman, even if she kissed like the world's most devoted Cyprian. Even if she had his body raging against every last modicum of decency he possessed.

Gareth took the tip of her other breast in his mouth and then painted lazy circles around her nipple before lightly catching it in his teeth and tugging. That earned him another moan, a tug on his hair that he felt in his ballocks, which were already drawn taut from thwarted desire. It had been too long since he'd been with a woman, and surely that was the reason this American Siren with her utter lack of morals had so entranced him. It was his body's primitive urges, seizing control of his rational, calm, ordered mind.

He licked and sucked, and she arched her back and offered herself up to him like some manner of pagan sacrifice in the moonlight, and he wanted to snatch her up in his arms and lay her down on sweetly scented grass and pleasure her in every way he knew until she was dripping for him. His other hand traveled with its own will, fisting in her skirts and lifting them higher, higher. Until he slid under the heavy weight of her gown and just one petticoat and felt the warmth of her skin burning through her drawers. His fingers moved unerringly to the slit, wanting to see if she was wet, needing to touch her there, to stroke her.

To make her come.

He parted the opening of her drawers, and it was easy because her leg was still hooked on his hip, opening her to him, his fingers free to glide inside for the first kiss of her hot, silken flesh.

And dear God, sweet Christ, she was wet. So perfectly, wonderfully soaked.

"Oh, Robert," she gasped out, jerking into his touch, offering herself to him eagerly.

But that was when the ardor finally began to die.

Because she'd said the wrong name, another man's. Her wanton kisses, her soft sighs, her throaty moans, her wet cunny, her lack of undergarments, hadn't been meant for him at all. None of it had.

Bloody hell, she thought he was someone else.

In that wretched moment as he jerked his hand from beneath her skirts, Gareth wished most fervently that he was.

CHAPTER 2

Something was amiss, but Lucy was so lost in the fog of passion that it took her addled mind a few seconds to recall how to function. But there was a difference in Robert, a sudden stiffness in his bearing.

He'd stopped touching her, dropping her gown as if it were a poisonous snake, jerking his mouth from her breast. He was withdrawing. Settling her away from him with hasty, measured motions that were at odds with the fiery lover he'd been not a minute before.

Had she done something wrong? Had she been too eager? Had she shocked him?

"Is something amiss?" she asked, wishing she could see his features, his gaze fully, but the moon had disappeared behind a cloud, rendering the night even darker than it had been when she'd first ventured to the gardens.

"Yes," he said succinctly, an angry hiss. "You seem to have mistaken me for another."

It wasn't the charmingly lilting Yorkshire accent of Robert the handsome footman she heard. But rather the crisp, neatly enunciated accent of a lord. A voice she recognized, in fact, because it had recently been cool and disapproving, directed at her.

She grasped at her bodice, pulling it frantically over her bare breasts, shock making her newly aware of the cool night air. "You're not Robert."

"Distinctly not, Miss Chartrand."

He sounded annoyed with her. Of course he did. The Earl of Rexingham despised her. He looked down his nose at her as if she were a worm who had just crawled out of the mud to vex him, and he had warned his sister to stay away from Lucy as if she were some manner of jezebel intent upon leading the poor girl down the path to depravity.

Which, given what she'd done with the man himself in the gardens, didn't seem an unreasonable assumption just now. Heat clawed up her throat, shame mingling with distress.

"What are you doing here, my lord?" she demanded, struggling with the tiny buttons on her bodice.

Her hands were trembling. Why had she decided not to wear a chemise? Why had she not called out to the man joining her in the moonlight before she'd kissed him?

And why had such a cold, haughty earl kissed her with such scorching passion?

He'd known it was her. He'd called her Miss Chartrand. Nothing made sense.

"I could ask the same of you, but the answer is readily apparent," he said, calmly straightening his own garments as she continued to wrestle her bodice into submission. "Pray enlighten me, who is Robert? One of the other guests? A stable lad? The head gardener?"

Her nostrils flared with irritation as she stuffed another button through its hole, noting the order of his questioning. "None of your business, my lord."

That she was able to keep her tone even and unaffected was a minor miracle. Inside, she was seething.

But not just seething. She was also in tumult. Because the Earl of Rexingham's kisses had affected her quite deeply. He had opened her bodice, kissed her breasts. His mouth had been on her nipples and his hand had been under her skirts, and she'd been ready to lie in the grass with him and let him have his wicked way. She had liked it, had wanted it.

In the darkness, he had been a lover she was prepared to welcome into her body, to give herself to, and she wouldn't have regretted it for a moment. She could acknowledge, if only to herself, that her feelings, the desire coursing through her, had been solely caused by the earl and not by the footman who had failed to meet her.

She hadn't any affection for Robert; he'd merely been handsome and convenient, and she'd fancied herself bold enough to use him for her plan. Apparently, he was also either perpetually tardy or inconstant. It hardly seemed to matter which one now. But she also hadn't been certain she'd be willing to allow things between them to progress any further than mere kisses.

The terrible truth lived and breathed inside her—she would have allowed it with Rexingham.

"I would say it is indeed my business, given what just occurred here," he said tightly, as if he couldn't bear to form words to describe the kisses, caresses, and mutual seduction they'd just shared.

"What just occurred," she repeated in a mocking tone, attempting to approximate his deep, pompous voice. "Do you mean to say your mouth on my breast?"

"Do cease being vulgar," he snapped.

She finished the final button, defiance rising with her irritation. "Why? You seemed to like it until a minute or so ago."

"Until you said the name of your lover," he pointed out. "So tell me, which man will I have to warn away from my future wife?"

Lucy choked. Sputtered. Choked some more.

"Future wife?" she managed to rasp.

"Yes, regretfully my lapse of judgment requires me to rectify matters." He was crisp, unaffected.

She wanted to scream, but that wouldn't be wise. Bringing all the Duke and Duchess of Bradford's guests down upon them wouldn't suit her plan. Not in the slightest.

"Consider yourself absolved of any need to *rectify matters*, as you say," she told him. "I have no wish to marry anyone, least of all a sanctimonious lord who can't even admit his hand was up my leg, parting my drawers and touching my—"

"Hold your uncivil tongue, madam," he interrupted curtly.

"What will you do if I don't?" she dared to ask, feeling mulish.

He had fooled her. She'd thought he was Robert, and instead, he'd been *better* than Robert before she had discovered who he truly was. He had kissed her until she'd been delirious with longing, had touched her and made her burn for him. Had turned her into a melting puddle of desire. And then he had opened his mouth and spoiled it all.

"Do you dare to challenge me?" he asked, as if no one else had ever done so before her.

And perhaps they hadn't. After all, he was the supercilious Earl of Rexingham, always above reproach. In his own mind, at least.

She tipped her head back in defiance, wishing she could see him better, but the blasted tiny moon was still nestled firmly behind a bank of clouds. "Yes, your high-and-mighty lordship, I do. You can't tell me to hold my tongue. You may be an earl, but I'm an American. You have no sovereignty over me."

"Unfortunately, I'm the man who is going to be your husband, and as such, I very much will have sovereignty over you," he said cooly. "You may as well accustom yourself to it now."

Lucy laughed. "I regretfully inform you that I'm not marrying anyone, Lord Rexingham. Particularly not choleric aristocrats who seem to confuse an innocent tryst in the moonlight with a proposal of marriage."

He had bent to retrieve his hastily discarded coat, and for a wild moment, she imagined what he would do if she simply fled from the gardens, racing away. Would he follow her? Pretend nothing had happened the next morning when they met at the breakfast sideboard?

But then she banished such notions as pure cowardice, beneath her. She wasn't afraid of the earl. He couldn't force her into marriage, regardless of how much he blustered.

He straightened, effortlessly shrugging into his coat. "Madam, nothing about what happened between us was innocent, and even an American without a bit of care for decorum or society would have to be a fool to think that this unfortunate incident will lead anywhere other than marriage. Lamentably, I might add, for I would sooner eat my hat than bind myself to a careless hoyden who frolics in gardens with unknown gentlemen."

"I thought you were Robert," she countered. "You were only unknown to me because you failed to tell me who you were."

"Perhaps I would have done so had you not thrown yourself at me and begun kissing me."

"Thrown myself at you?" she repeated, infuriated.

She realized, quite belatedly, that he wasn't entirely wrong. She had indeed thrown herself at him. But she'd thought he was Robert then. What was his excuse? He'd known who she was.

"How else would you describe barreling into me and clinging to me like a barnacle?" he asked.

A barnacle? Oh, now she wanted to throw something at his insufferable head. Pity she didn't have any weapons handy.

"You didn't seem to mind," she pointed out, remembering the way he had touched her, kissed her, unbuttoned her bodice.

Remembering the way his mouth had felt on her.

Heat washed over her again, her belly feeling as if it had tipped. She promptly tamped down the unwanted feelings.

"You took me by surprise. I can assure you that if I'd been given the proper time to defend myself against your improper advances, I would have been far less affected."

His voice was frigid now, but he hadn't been cold when he'd been kissing her. And Lucy didn't know why, but it nettled her that he was acting as if she were anathema to him. She longed to argue with him further, to make him admit he had enjoyed himself as much as she had. But what would be the use in such a concession? It wouldn't change anything.

And she very much needed to persuade Rexingham that this night was best forgotten. All he needed were some pointed reminders that no one else knew about this mistake other than the two of them. And that no one else ever needed to know. It could be their mutual, very-well-kept secret.

"Forgive me, my lord," she bit out, the effort to gentle her tone almost painful. "What happened was a mistake, an unfortunate lapse in judgment. However, no one else need ever hear of it. I can assure you I won't leave this garden carrying any tales."

"I'll speak with your mother in the morning," he said, quite as if she hadn't spoken at all.

"No," she denied frantically, "you won't."

Mother would be ridiculously pleased to receive an offer of marriage from an earl. It was her greatest dream to see her daughters married into the English aristocracy. Unfortunately for Mother, however, her daughters didn't share that ambition.

The clouds chose that moment to part, and silvery light illuminated the harsh angles of his handsome face—the patrician cheekbones, the strong jaw, and proud chin. He wasn't a difficult man to look upon. Pity he quite ruined the effect whenever he opened his mouth.

"You may not have any honor, Miss Chartrand," he said then, his tone as cutting as a blade, "but I do, and mine cannot allow what has been done to go unanswered. Despite the fact that you're the last woman in the world I would wish to saddle myself with, I'm afraid our actions this evening have left me with no choice."

He was intolerable.

"I'd sooner jump out of a moving train than marry you," she blurted.

A small, mocking smile curved the lips that had so recently been on hers. "Regretfully, you'll need to reconcile yourself to your fate. I trust there won't be any further trysts with Robert, whomever he may be. If nothing else, circumspection is a quality I require in my future wife."

Did the man's stubbornness know no end? She wondered if he could hear any voices that weren't his own.

Lucy surrendered to her frustration and stamped her foot. "I am *not* your future wife."

He offered her his arm. "Come along, then. The hour is growing late, and the longer we linger in this garden, the greater our risk of discovery and further scandal."

She glared at him—not that he could see it in the darkness, but oh, how she wished he could. "I'm not going anywhere with you."

"I'm afraid you must." His voice was tight, as if he were struggling to control emotion.

Briefly, she wondered what he had been doing, wandering in the gardens so late. It seemed highly unlike his proper self. And of course, just her misfortune that he had been. Suspicion bloomed, sudden and fierce.

"Do you need my family's fortune?" she asked sharply.

Heaven knew she'd been chased by many a fortune hunter. Rexingham didn't truly seem the type. He hadn't been unctuous, nor had he flattered her endlessly. He had made his true opinion of her more than clear.

"Of course not. The Claremont family has always been remarkably adept at cultivating wealth and keeping it."

"Then there is no need for you to keep insisting upon this marriage nonsense."

"There is every need, Miss Chartrand, as I've already explained repeatedly ad nauseam." He took her hand in his and tucked it into the crook of his arm in a proprietary fashion.

The action took her so much by surprise that she didn't think to wrest herself from his grasp until it was too late, and he'd clamped a hand over hers, keeping it trapped in place. His hand was warm, and that inconvenient spark of aware-ness shot through her again. She liked his touch. Unfortu-nately, she didn't like *him*.

Lucy cleared her throat. "Lord Rexingham, if you will only listen to reason."

He began walking, pulling her along as if she were a little dog on a leash with no choice but to follow. "I'm reasonably certain nothing that comes out of your mouth will have a drop of reason attached to it."

How smug he was. How superior.

She stopped on the gravel path, forcing him to pause as

16

well. "It's a miracle you've lasted this long without someone throwing you in front of a carriage."

"Ah, Miss Chartrand, you warm the cockles of my heart with your kind words."

She would have thought sarcasm beneath him. But apparently, like those wicked kisses, the Earl of Rexingham possessed hidden facets.

"You have a heart?" she asked before she could think better of it. "I'm shocked, my lord."

He chuckled, surprising her again. The sound was low and velvety, and it made an unwanted frisson of desire unfurl within her.

"Touché, madam." The earl started moving again, pulling her reluctantly with him.

"I'm not marrying you," she warned him as they moved toward the looming shadow of the manor house.

But the earl simply continued on, his long-legged strides making it difficult for her to keep up with him, quickly rendering her breathless. By the time they reached the doors to the library, a steady rain had begun to fall, and further protest on her part was moot.

GARETH TURNED to the dripping American woman on his arm, feeling oddly detached. He was going to have to marry her, regardless of her vociferous protests. It didn't matter that she'd been meeting someone else in the gardens, that she likely wasn't a virgin, that she was as polished and countess-like as a charwoman. He had taken liberties with her.

Shocking liberties.

He'd given in to his base lust, even when he'd known to do so was ruinous.

"I'm sorry about what happened in the gardens," Miss

Chartrand told him quietly, her tone and demeanor softened from the determined virago in the moonlight who had been adamant she wouldn't wed him. "But surely you must realize the necessity of keeping this between the two of us. No one else ever need know."

That explained the sudden sea change. Perhaps the cunning minx believed she could cozen him into doing her bidding if she employed a different method of persuasion.

"On the contrary," he countered, dashing the rain from first one coat sleeve and then the other. "Your mother needs to be informed. I'll do so directly and in private, following breakfast. I would have preferred to ask your father for your hand in the customary way, but his absence leaves me with no other choice."

Unbidden, the memory of asking for Anthea's hand rose in his mind, unpleasant and bitter. How eager he had been then, a naïve fool who had stupidly believed he had a life of happy contentedness ahead of him. He had suspected Anthea's reserved nature had been down to her lack of experience, her gently bred sensibilities. He'd soon learned differently.

"No." Miss Chartrand shivered. "You won't do anything of the sort."

Her accent was strangely endearing. It was all wrong, and yet it flowed over him like water. And no wonder she was taking a chill. Her lack of undergarments and thin bodice were precious little protection from the rains that had begun to lash them on their way back inside. In the low lamplight of the library, he noted against his will the way the wet silk clung to her skin.

By God, her nipples were hard. Pointing directly at him like a taunt that stole his breath and robbed his mouth of all moisture. He knew what those nipples tasted like, how they felt, randy and beaded in his mouth. He knew she liked when he used his teeth.

He shifted his stance, attempting to ease the sudden ache in his trousers, and reminded himself he was a gentleman. "You're cold. There appears to be something of a fire left in the grate. Let's have our talk there if we must."

For in truth, he didn't want to linger with her. Didn't want to converse. Every second in her ridiculously erotic presence was a temptation he found increasingly impossible to resist. But his sense of honor led him, his compass.

"I fear lingering here with you will only make the circumstances worse," Miss Chartrand told him.

Wise girl.

But they were well beyond any chance of extricating themselves from this mess unattached. How odd to think he was looking at the next Countess of Rexingham. After his disastrous marriage with Anthea had ended upon her death, he had vowed never to wed again. And yet, here he found himself.

"Come," he said implacably, taking her hand in his.

Instead of wrenching away from him as he'd supposed she might, Miss Chartrand laced her fingers with his. It was instant, perhaps instinctive. And it shouldn't have made a strange knot of some unfamiliar emotion rise in his throat, but it did.

They moved to the fire, which had been banked for the night—Sherborne Manor was a drafty affair, even in summer. A pleasant warmth still emanated from the coals, but it was Miss Chartrand's hand in his that filled Gareth with heat. He released it at once, telling himself he needed to have a care for propriety, even if he was marrying her. He couldn't afford to lose control again, lest he end up tupping her on the library floor.

"The fire ought to take away the chill," he said with forced civility. "You're soaked to the skin."

She had been soaked elsewhere too, and it hadn't had a thing to do with the rain. But he instantly dismissed that unworthy thought.

"You needn't fret over me," Miss Chartrand said. "I can see to myself perfectly well."

"Is that what landed you in the garden, engaging in a tryst?" he asked before he could think better of it.

Jealousy rose, sharp and strong. Jealousy over Robert, whomever he was. She'd been waiting for another man. Another man had been the intended recipient of her passionate kisses, her soft, sweetly scented curves. Had she planned to lie with the man, out of doors?

A sudden image rose in his mind, of her on her back, her skirts rucked to her waist. But it wasn't a stranger Gareth saw between her thighs, fucking her deeply, making her moan and writhe as she reached her peak. It was himself.

"I don't see that it's any concern of yours, Lord Rexingham," she said stiffly.

"It is my concern," he countered. "You'll be my wife. It's my duty to be informed."

She gave a small laugh. "Again with this silly nonsense. I've told you that I have no intention of marrying. Not you or anyone else."

"Who is Robert?" he asked again, hating himself for the question. Wanting to know and yet also needing to remain ignorant for the sake of his pride.

Miss Chartrand huffed a small sigh, and he found himself admiring her profile. "A footman, if you must know."

"A servant. How very American of you, my dear." He spoke with a sangfroid he didn't feel, and he prided himself on it.

Gareth wasn't a man who was easily provoked. Not any longer. He'd long since lost his ability to feel.

But he didn't relish the notion of taking a wife who preferred to dally with those in service. No help for it now. He'd compromised her. He'd touched her cunny. And he'd wanted to do far more.

Still wanted to, in fact.

"Do you think a man is less worthy by sheer virtue of the accident of his birth?" she asked sharply.

The hour was late. Gareth wasn't prepared to argue primogeniture.

"I think a man who waits until after midnight for an assignation with a woman is far from a gentleman," he offered mildly.

She turned, her vivid gaze connecting with his. "What does that say about you?"

Her eyes were green. He'd noticed them before—a quite unique, unusual shade, complemented by her rich mahogany hair.

"I wasn't meeting anyone for an assignation," he answered honestly. "I was taking the air."

Her eyes narrowed. "At this late hour?"

"I couldn't sleep."

He'd been overset after a nightmare, but he wasn't going to tell her that. He suffered them far less frequently now than he had immediately after Anthea's death. The handful of intervening years had helped to heal, if not cure, him. The chill night air always had a calming, bracing effect in such circumstances.

Unless one was set upon by an American heiress who could bring a man to his knees with only a kiss.

The thought of her tongue in his mouth made a sharp pang of need surge through Gareth. He had seen her in the gardens, of course. Had known it was her. He ought to have made haste in the opposite direction. And yet, he had followed her.

She was studying him in that intent way she had, looking far too closely at him, as if she could hear his forbidden thoughts. "You knew it was me in the garden."

It wasn't a question. He'd given himself away, calling her by name.

He inclined his head. "I did."

"But you don't like me."

He liked certain parts of her too much, and that was the problem. But as with the reason for his restlessness, he wouldn't divulge the information.

"I don't know you well enough to dislike you, Miss Chartrand," he said politely instead.

She laughed again, and it was a glorious sound—rich and unfettered. He wanted to hear it more.

"You misunderstand me, my lord. What I meant to say was that I fail to comprehend why you would kiss me as you did when you knew it was me. I've seen the way you look down your nose at me, rather as if I were an insect with the temerity to find my way into your bowl of soup."

He almost laughed at that ridiculous analogy of hers. "I can't say I've ever found an insect in my soup."

"You still haven't answered my question," she pointed out.

"I didn't hear one."

"Why did you kiss me the way you did?"

Blast.

"Because you're a remarkably proficient kisser, and I briefly lost control," he said tautly, irked at having to make the confession.

Irked too at how easily he had lost control with her. He'd thought himself above such an appalling lack of restraint. He was in Yorkshire at a country house party where he was squiring his innocent sister about. The potential damage his recklessness could do to Bette's reputation was of paramount concern.

"That's a compliment, I reckon," she said, still watching him closely, as if she were newly curious about him.

And he began to realize that Miss Lucy Chartrand was far more than the flighty fribble he'd originally supposed her to be. She was intelligent. Far too clever and interested in everyone around her.

"Not one most gently bred ladies aspire to," he said cuttingly.

That was true, but he hated the way she turned away from him at last, staring into the dying embers of the fire. It felt as if he had lost something significant, and now he was desperate to have it back.

"Fortunately, I'm no gently bred lady," she said softly. "Kissing is an enjoyable art."

He almost swallowed his tongue at the savage bolt of lust that went through him. He wanted to kiss her again. Wanted those plump, pouting lips of hers on him everywhere. Especially on his cock. But that was wrong—a gentleman didn't make such demands. He knew better.

"I trust you'll temper the art, as you call it," he managed, "given our understanding."

"Not with the marriage nonsense again." She issued another sigh. "Go to bed, my lord. Forget you ever saw me in the gardens. I'll do the same."

He *couldn't* forget. Not the needy moans she'd made. Not the slick, velvet heat of her sex. Not the pebbled buds of her nipples on his tongue.

He cleared his throat. "Impossible. I hold myself to the standards of a gentleman, Miss Chartrand. Without honor, one has nothing."

"My lord, I understand your concern, but this argument grows wearisome."

It did. He was going to marry her, and that was that. Nothing she could say would dissuade him.

"I'm afraid you'll have to accept your fate," he told her.

Miss Chartrand had turned back to him again, and her emerald eyes were fairly snapping with annoyance. It occurred to him, with sudden clarity, that he wasn't going to win this particular argument with her in any way save one.

"That's very lordly of you, but I'm afraid—"

He silenced the rest of her objections with his lips. It was a mistake. He recognized that the moment she sank against him, her body melding to his in lush surrender. She opened instantly, and he couldn't resist sweeping his tongue inside to taste her again. He told himself he was doing what was right, proving to Miss Chartrand that an offer of marriage was a necessity. But he was also doing what was very wrong, what felt wicked and sinful and like the most potent aphrodisiac he'd ever known.

His hands were moving, touching her. How could he not? Running up and down the hollow at the small of her back, traveling over the shapely natural curve of her waist. Her tongue moved sinuously against his, nary a hint of objection. He would make her forget the damned footman, he thought. She knew whose mouth was on hers now, and she was responding every bit as beautifully as before.

But then another thought stole into his mind, as unwanted as the reminder she hadn't realized she'd been kissing him in the gardens. He lifted his head, staring down at her in the low light, drinking in her bold American beauty, so different from the English ladies of his acquaintance.

"Are you in love with him?" he asked, hating the notion.

She blinked. "With whom?"

"The footman," he gritted. "Richard."

"Robert," she corrected, and then her tongue stole over

her lower lip, as if savoring the taste of him there, on her mouth. "And no. I scarcely know him."

He ought to have been appalled at her revelation, horrified to discover she'd gone to meet a servant in the moonlight whom she'd likely never shared a meaningful conversation with. What manner of woman was she to do so?

A brazen one.

Her personality was vastly different from Anthea's cold aloofness, from her resentment toward him, her eventual anger and hatred.

Miss Chartrand was refreshing. Intoxicating. He could get drunk on her kisses alone.

He took her mouth again without saying a word. Words ceased to matter, ceased to exist. She twined her arms around his neck, rubbing against him like a cat, and he felt the pointed buds of her nipples through his coat. Madness overtook him. Sheer, animal lust. He guided her backward, to a piece of furniture in the shadows. She kissed him as if she were starved for him, nipping at his lip. They sank onto the couch as one, her beneath him, Gareth atop her. There was scarcely sufficient room, but he didn't care.

His rigid cock was trapped between them, longing for release.

More, more, more.

That was what he needed, what he wanted. Desire robbed him of any capacity for rational thought. And it was worse now than it had been in the gardens, his body still primed as a pump, ready for her, desperate for her. He could fuck her on this couch in the Duke of Bradford's library, and he wouldn't feel a hint of remorse. He could move her skirts higher, out of his way.

And then his hand was doing it, obeying his wildly flitting

thoughts. Grasping a handful of silk and dragging it up to her knee.

But no, this wasn't right. What the hell was he doing? He had to think of his sister. Of his honor.

Gareth yanked his lips from hers and tore himself away from her pliant curves, leaving her on the couch looking thoroughly kissed.

He tugged at his coat, willing his erection to abate. "I'll speak with your mother in the morning," he informed her with a remarkable amount of aplomb for a man who'd been on the verge of spending in his trousers.

With a bow, he quit the room.

CHAPTER 3

"I think I'm in a bit of trouble," Lucy told her sister. Madeline had just bustled into her guest chamber so they could have their customary chat before breakfast, and not a moment too soon. Lucy had been pacing and fretting after a night spent tossing and turning, with very little sleep. This, she blamed on the Earl of Rexingham, who kissed like a sinner but spoke like a vicar.

"You're always in trouble," Madeline said breezily, unconcerned. "It may as well be your middle name, dearest. What have you done now?"

Lucy winced. "I agreed to meet a footman in the gardens last night."

"Mother will be horrified," her sister drawled, dropping into an overstuffed chair by the hearth. "What happened?"

Lucy joined her, suddenly needing to sit. "The footman failed to appear."

"Well, that's disappointing." Madeline sighed wistfully. "If you were in the gardens alone, how did you get yourself into trouble?"

"Because someone else was there," she admitted, her

27

cheeks going hot as she remembered the shameless way she'd thrown herself into the earl's arms.

And the way she'd responded to him later in the library, lying on a couch with him atop her.

"You're blushing," Madeline said with renewed interest. "I didn't think you were capable of it. Tell me, who is the someone who was in the gardens?"

It was true that Lucy tended to be the bolder of the two of them. She read torrid novels and not much could shock her or shake her. The Earl of Rexingham had, however. As had her reaction to him.

"The Earl of Rexingham," she admitted.

"The priggish one who looks down his nose at us as if we're costermongers trying to sell him spoiled fruit?"

Lucy might have laughed if she weren't feeling so on edge about the earl's determination to marry her. "That's the one."

"What did he do, admonish you for sneaking out after you should have been asleep?" Madeline chuckled at her own joke.

"He kissed me," she blurted. "And…more."

Her sister's eyebrows shot up. "What does that mean?"

"It means I wasn't wearing many undergarments, and he…we…" Lucy's words trailed away, her face going hotter.

"Did he bed you?" Madeline wanted to know.

"Madeline." Her ears were on fire, and a different heat entirely was creeping over her, blossoming from low in her belly, as she remembered his fingers parting her drawers and touching her.

"Well, did he?" her sister demanded, unmoved by her protest.

"No." Lucy sighed heavily. "But he seems to think that what happened between us means he needs to speak with Mother and offer to marry me."

"Oh dear," Madeline said.

"The whole point of meeting the footman in the gardens was to avoid marriage," Lucy said. "Not to find myself engaged to an earl. Particularly not one as aloof and proper as Rexingham. He'd never allow me to start my cosmetics business."

He hadn't been proper when he'd been kissing her. Or when his mouth had been on her bare breasts. The memory made her nipples tighten into achy buds beneath her corset. No, she wouldn't think about that now. There was nothing to recommend the man aside from his wickedly skilled kisses.

"Something happened between the two of you," Madeline said pointedly, almost as if she were privy to Lucy's thoughts. "Surely he wasn't being so very proper then."

Sisters, she thought glumly.

"I don't want to talk about it. I'd rather come up with a plan for keeping him from speaking with Mother."

"We could hit him over the head with something," Madeline suggested unhelpfully. "Or lock him in a room. How about both?"

"I don't think we could keep him locked in a room for the rest of the house party," Lucy said wryly. "And I'd rather not cause him any injuries. I don't want to maim him. I just don't want to marry him either."

"Hmm." Madeline tapped on her chin. "Have you told Lord Rexingham that you don't want to marry him?"

"Of course I have."

"And what did he say?"

He had kissed her and lain on the couch with her, and she had never wanted it to end.

"He disagreed with me," she said instead. "Going on about his honor as a gentleman."

"Why would meeting the footman in the gardens help you avoid marriage?" Madeline queried.

"I was hoping he might help to ruin me so thoroughly

that Mother would abandon all hope of securing a suitable match for me," she admitted.

The plan had sounded better to her when she had conceived it. At the time, she hadn't expected for it to go so hopelessly awry.

"But the earl ruined you instead." Madeline gave her arm a soothing pat. "I'm afraid you've done exactly what Mother hoped."

Lucy closed her eyes and leaned her head back against the chair. "You're meant to be helping me find a solution to my problem, not confirming what I already know."

"How did you end up kissing Lord Rexingham instead of the footman?" Madeline asked.

Lucy opened her eyes again to pin her sister with a glare. "I mistook him for Robert. Unfortunately, he didn't inform me of my error until things had progressed."

"Oh dear," Madeline repeated.

"That's the second time you've said that."

"Yes, well, sister darling, you've managed to land yourself in rather a lot of trouble with your latest scrape."

Lucy had created a seemingly endless string of minor scandals, it was true, both in New York City and abroad. But their mother had refused to relent.

"Unfortunately, it's not the sort of trouble that will force all Mother's marital aspirations for me to die a swift and easy death," she grumbled. "It's the opposite of what I intended."

"She'll be thrilled," Madeline agreed, wincing.

"You see? I need to do something before he goes to her and spoils everything."

Because Lucy didn't want to marry the earl, regardless of how skilled he was at kissing and…other things.

"Maybe you should try speaking with him this morning," her sister suggested. "When did he say he would seek out Mother?"

"After breakfast."

"Oh d—"

"Don't say it again, if you please," Lucy interrupted her older sister. "You've already said it twice, and if you say it a third time, I just may throw myself out of the window."

"You'd land in the rosebushes, darling," Madeline said, grinning. "I don't think it would be a glorious fall, considering all those thorns. If you didn't break your neck, of course."

Lucy found herself smiling back at her sister, despite the gravity of the situation. "If I broke my neck, I wouldn't have to worry about marrying the earl."

"And if you broke your neck, I wouldn't have a sister to advise against jumping out of windows. Marriage to the earl would be a far preferable fate and much less gory."

"Ever the voice of reason, my dear." Lucy rose from her chair, glancing at the mantel clock. "I suppose I should try to find Rexingham before I run out of time."

Madeline stood as well, slanting her a saucy look. "If the earl is that skilled at kissing, marrying him wouldn't be a hardship."

Lucy thought of his superciliousness and shuddered. "Yes, it would. Wish me luck, sister."

"Good luck," Madeline said. "I have a feeling you may need it."

GARETH STARED AT HIS REFLECTION, adjusting his neck cloth, which suddenly felt far too tight. He bore the grim countenance of a man about to meet his fate at the business end of a hangman's noose, he thought.

Quite appropriate.

His gut was curdled with dread. He'd escaped one miser-

31

able, unhappy union, and now he was about to mire himself in another one. He was a careful man—he had always lived above reproach. And yet, he'd been the cause for both marriages.

With Anthea, it had been obligation that had spurred him. Their families had expected them to make a match, and he'd offered for her hand to please his father. He'd been too young and stupid to recognize her coolness toward him as anything less than politeness and refinement.

On their wedding night, she had lain there stiffly, covers pulled to her chin, begging him to do what he must and leave her be, her words and movements made sluggish from a recent dose of laudanum. Time hadn't altered her opinion of the marriage bed or him, and she'd only grown steadily more dependent upon opium over the years. Until eventually, she had shriveled away into a husk of herself, and the laudanum had claimed her.

Anthea had been correct, however. He was a base, licentious beast of a man. And now the appetite he'd never been able to quell, regardless of how hard he tried, had landed him in a most precarious position. He never should have kissed Miss Chartrand back last night. He shouldn't have taken her in his arms, unbuttoned her bodice. He shouldn't have lifted her skirts.

But he had, and now he would pay the forfeit by seeking out her mother, as if he were a green lad who'd been carried away by his first kiss. Perhaps he hadn't the last time he'd offered for a woman, but this time, he damn well knew better—knew the miseries that awaited a man in a marriage. And yet, he'd done what he had with Miss Chartrand anyway.

Worse, he wanted to do it again.

He cleared his throat and adjusted his trousers, which felt as snug as his damned necktie. A deep breath, another hateful glare at himself in the mirror, and then he left his chamber. His sister, Bette, would no doubt find it desperately amusing that he was marrying one of the wild American heiresses he'd warned her not to associate with at this house party.

What a fool he was. A fool with honor. Which necessitated this most unwanted conversation with Mrs. William Chartrand, a preening peacock of a woman whose mission in life was apparently to secure her daughters aristocratic husbands. He was about to aid her with that, much to his dismay. He made his way down the hall to the grand staircase, descending with an ominous prescience that wouldn't relent its stranglehold on him.

Just the thought of taking Mrs. Chartrand aside for the uncomfortable conversation that would ensue made Gareth faintly queasy.

"Lord Rexingham."

The familiar voice—throaty and husky and not at all gently bred, complete with American accent—reached him as he strode past a partially opened door. And there she was, Miss Lucy Chartrand, hovering at the threshold of a sitting room, looking even more alluring than she had in the moonlight where she'd gone to seduce a footman. That fact still rankled—he couldn't lie to himself.

"Miss Chartrand," he greeted with as much cheer as he could muster.

Scarcely any.

What was she doing, hiding in a sitting room? He could only hope she wasn't lying in wait for more of the male Sherborne Manor servants.

"Could I speak with you, please?" she asked, casting a furtive glance around the hall.

The hour was still quite early, and their fellow guests weren't yet thronging to the dining room for their morning

33

repast. No one else was about. Not that it mattered. He was marrying her anyway.

"I was on my way to breakfast," he said, not trusting himself to linger in a room alone with her.

"Please," she entreated.

He sighed heavily, casting another glance around. Not even a servant about. Such was the nature of the Duke and Duchess of Bradford's household. The domestics were so efficient that they were almost invisible.

Gareth entered the sitting room against his better judgment, closing the door at his back before moving to the opposite end of the room, near a window. He could distract himself by looking outside if necessary. A safe distance from her, and he wouldn't be tempted to touch.

And tempted, he was. Because she was wearing a gown of blue silk that clung to her curves in the most mouthwatering way, her mahogany hair was woven into a Grecian plait with small curls free to frame her face, and her green eyes were blazing with determination.

"You can't approach my mother," she said.

He tugged at the end of his coat sleeve and brushed away an imaginary speck of lint. "This argument grows tedious, Miss Chartrand. I've already explained what necessitates offering for your hand."

"Stuff your honor," she said, swishing across the room to him. "No one knows what happened last night but the two of us and my sister, and no one else ever needs to know."

Dear God, she'd told her sister. He felt like a ravening brute.

"It isn't my intention to tell your mother what has happened," he forced out. "I'm merely asking for your hand as we previously discussed."

"No." She stopped before him, bringing with her the scent of roses. "That's impossible. My mother will be overjoyed at the prospect of my marrying an earl. But I don't have any intention of marrying at all."

In the morning light, he saw specks of gold and gray in her eyes. His hands itched to find her waist, to pull her against him. His mouth burned with the memory of her lips beneath it. He wanted her, and he hated himself for it. There was a bewitching eroticism to Miss Lucy Chartrand that he could neither deny nor resist. She hadn't spurned his kisses, his touch. She had liked them both, even after she'd discovered he wasn't her footman. The knowledge filled him with fire.

Dangerous fire.

"Why?" he made himself ask her, genuinely curious at her adamant vow she wanted nothing to do with marriage.

"Because I want to be free," she said. "Free to do whatever I want, whenever I want. I want control of my fortune, not for it to be handed off to my husband. And I want to have a business of my own one day."

Her response surprised him. He had expected a host of other reasons. Hadn't expected this obviously spoiled woman with a small fortune in diamonds currently clasped at her throat would think about something so plebian as money, nor that she would want to work to earn more of it. She'd likely been raised with the finest of everything. The Chartrand wealth was infamous, if regrettably new. Her father was a railroad magnate who hailed from a family that had already been flush with money from real estate investments. And a business of her own? He'd never heard of the like from a society lady.

"If you want reassurance your dowry will remain yours, I'll be happy to provide it," he said stiffly. "I've funds aplenty."

His marriage with Anthea had brought him a small fortune, it was true, but Gareth had thrown himself into making his estates profitable after his father's death. He had worked tirelessly to rebuild the coffers his predecessors had so soundly drained. Doing so had proven the perfect distraction from his unhappy marriage.

"Even if you'd be willing to provide me with that reassurance, I'm afraid it doesn't change the fact that I don't want to marry you," Miss Chartrand said.

He smiled, and not without bitterness. "You wouldn't be the first woman who didn't want to marry me, my dear. But that's rather a moot point. It's out of our hands now."

"You really are the most frustrating man."

Gareth remained unmoved by her exasperation. "And you are the most frustrating woman. Only think of how well matched we are."

"You can't force me to marry you, you know."

He was beginning to feel insulted. "I wouldn't dream of using force. I should hope marriage to me isn't that horrific a prospect."

"It isn't you. It's marriage itself."

"So it wasn't a quiet elopement you were hoping for with the footman?" he asked, unable to help himself.

A becoming flush crept over her cheekbones, painting them a pretty shade of pink. "It isn't any of your concern what I was hoping for, my lord."

"Forgive me for wanting to become better acquainted with the inner workings of my future wife's mind."

She let out an irritated sigh, something she'd done quite a bit of in his presence. "I'm *not* your future wife."

"Would you prefer for me to announce to our fellow guests, your mother included, that last night we came perilously close to fornication in both the library and the garden?" he asked cheerfully.

Her mouth dropped open, and for a moment, she was apparently speechless. And then she found her voice at last.

"Are you blackmailing me, Lord Rexingham?" she demanded, sounding outraged.

"I rather think I am," he admitted, astounded at himself.

Clearly, Miss Lucy Chartrand brought out the worst in him.

"That's diabolical," she accused.

It was. He shrugged, not bothering to deny it. He'd never been the sort of man who despoiled innocents. Not that he was entirely certain Miss Lucy Chartrand was innocent. He rather suspected she was the opposite. But she was an unmarried female with whom he had taken unacceptable liberties, and he refused to bend on the matter of his honor and the risk his actions posed to Bette.

"I'll have a contract drawn up for your approval," he said.

"I don't understand." Her brow furrowed. "Surely you don't want to marry me. You don't even *like* me. I know you told your sister to keep her distance from my distasteful influence."

Gareth was going to have to speak with Bette about her candor.

"I didn't say your influence was distasteful," he countered. "I said it was unsuitable."

Her chin went up. "Was that meant to somehow ameliorate the sting?"

"It was a clarification."

She glared at him, and the mad urge to kiss her again rose within him. Her indignation was strangely rousing. She appalled him and fascinated him all at once, this bold American woman he'd ruined.

"If you find me so objectionable, why marry me?"

"Because I was two seconds from taking you like a common doxy," he gritted. "My treatment of you was reprehensible. I must make amends, and there's only one means of doing so. Regretfully, that is making you my wife. I'm no more interested in marrying you than you are in marrying me, but we've progressed well beyond the bounds of polite society. And you may not have a sense of honor, Miss Chartrand, but I most assuredly do. And while marriage is as unpalatable to me as drinking a glass of sand, I'm also aware I need an heir."

She pressed a hand over her heart, and he noted the sapphires and diamonds winking from her slender fingers, more evidence of her family's ostentatious American fortune. "Your proposal is surely the most romantic one I've ever heard, Lord Rexingham. How could I possibly refuse you?"

Her lovely voice was steeped in sarcasm, and he could admit it was sarcasm he was owed. But if she expected him to play the knight gallant, she was doomed for disappointment. He was a man guided by pragmatism, duty, and honor. Unfortunately, he also possessed an unwanted appetite for the pleasures of the flesh, which had proven his downfall. This bold minx had somehow eroded his capacity for self-control.

One press of her lips to his was all it had taken.

He never should have wandered into the gardens. He shouldn't have followed her. And he most certainly should have thrust her far from him when she'd thrown herself into his arms.

"Allow me to rephrase, Miss Chartrand. Your primary objection to marriage appears to be that you don't want a husband to rule over your fortune. I've already reassured you I have no such intention. You can keep your money and sovereignty over it. Having already suffered one abysmal marriage, I'm hardly desirous of making you miserable. I promise to be considerate and polite, to avoid burdening you overly with my beastly desires, and to allow you to carry on as you like after giving me an heir.

Discreetly, of course, and preferably not with the domestics."

"I'm not certain the second proposal was an improvement over the first," she said coolly.

Had he ever met a more vexing woman?

"Then I suppose I've no choice but to attempt a third."

"I don't think you should."

He reached for her, planting his hands on her narrow waist as he had been longing, pulling her into him. She crashed into his chest, rose-scented and maddeningly beautiful. Gareth took advantage of her momentary surprise and lowered his head, sealing his lips over hers.

The Earl of Rexingham was kissing her.

Again.

Lucy's hands fluttered to his shoulders. She should push him away, but she didn't want to. All she wanted to do was hold him close. To keep him there. Was this his idea of a proposal? If so, she had to admit that it was far preferable to all the others that had preceded it.

His shoulders were so delightfully broad and strong. He wasn't an idle lord, and she had no notion of what physical exertion he involved himself in, but she appreciated the effect. Even if he had just delivered arrogant, insulting proposals, even if he disapproved of her, and even if he spoke with dispassionate composure, when he kissed her, he managed to make her forget everything and everyone else.

His tongue was in her mouth, a hot, velvet glide, and she couldn't seem to tamp down the moan rising in her throat, nor the desire unfurling within her, answering him. If he would only kiss her and never speak again, she might be persuaded to accept his proposal. Her body certainly liked his well enough. It was merely her mind that objected to any entanglements lasting longer than a tryst.

He lifted his head, and she almost cried out at the loss of his lips on hers.

"We'll suit well, I think," he said, a rather smug note in his voice that made her want to slap him and then kiss him again.

His head dipped, his mouth claiming hers before she could do the former, and the latter once more ruled her thoughts. His mouth was smooth yet firm, demanding and coaxing. And he wasn't wrong. They did suit in this fashion. She'd kissed others before him, but she'd never kissed anyone who made her feel this way. Restless and desperate for more. She could kiss him forever and never grow weary of it.

But kissing and marrying were two separate matters entirely, and she mustn't forget it. Kissing was pleasurable. Binding herself to a man she scarcely knew, who could go back on his word if he chose, would be entirely the opposite. She would summon a greater resistance to his deeply persuasive mouth soon. If only she could gather her wits long enough to do it.

But her fingers were sinking of their own volition into that solidly hewn muscle trapped beneath the layers of his coat and shirt. His tongue was hot and sleek, and his hands were not just gripping her waist now, but caressing it, as if she were something luxurious and rare, something to be savored.

He moved them abruptly, and suddenly, she was on a seat built into the window, her bottom on a tufted cushion, cool glass panes at her back. His fingers caught her skirts, grasping and raising, and he insinuated himself between her legs, wedging himself there as if it were where he belonged as he lavished kisses on her lips, along her jaw, stringing a hot line of them to her ear.

It was too much, just as it had been last night.

It was not enough.

Someone moaned and sighed, the sound foreign even as she realized it had come from her. Her skirts lifted, hems brushing over her calves, past her knees. This was far more perilous than their tryst last night had been. They were in a sitting room at breakfast when their fellow guests were about to descend and avail themselves of their host and hostess's lavish serving board. And yet, she couldn't seem to bring herself to care.

He cupped her breast in his other hand, fingers molding around her flesh even through her undergarments, thumb brushing over the place where her nipple hid behind her corset. She wanted suddenly to be free of the abundance of boning and linen and silk. Wanted his touch on her bare skin. Wanted him to bring her skirts to her waist. To find the slit in her drawers. To fit himself against her and take her here on the window seat where anyone could see.

"Do you see, Miss Chartrand," he murmured against her throat, "the necessity in marriage?"

She wanted to deny him, but his hand had found its way above her garter, and he was caressing her thigh, his heat searing her through the fine silk of her drawers.

He lifted his head, his mysterious blue gaze, ordinarily so cool and aloof and yet now blazing with passionate fire, meeting hers. "Your answer, if you please."

His voice was low and deep, and she was briefly fascinated by the harsh angle of his jaw, the sculpture of his mouth. He was freshly shaven, and he smelled like soap and musky citrus with a hint of pine. She wanted to breathe him in, to bury her face in his neck and inhale.

They stared at each other, their bodies entwined, an intimate air between them that shouldn't have belonged to strangers. His breath coasted over her lips, his eyes searing in their intensity. His hair was perfectly arranged, this stern, brooding, elegant lord. He terrified her and thrilled her, and she should sooner leap from the window behind her than allow this dangerous game to proceed any further.

"I do believe you're trying to seduce me into agreeing to be your wife," she said breathlessly, finding her voice, her wits, at last.

"You seemed to require additional persuasion," he said, his lips remaining a firm, unforgiving line.

His smiles were rare, and he carried with him an air of sadness she'd mistaken for frigidity. He'd mentioned a previous marriage, one that had been unhappy. She'd known he was a widower because Madeline delighted in knowing everything there was to know about everyone, and their mother was an inveterate gossip. For the first time since the madness of the moonlight, she found herself wondering what life as this austere man's wife would be like.

But that was foolish, wild, nonsensical thinking. She didn't want to marry him. Until last night, he'd made his opinion of her more than clear. He only felt obligated by honor. Attraction was not a foundation for a marriage, and neither was lust.

And yet, disturbing, unwanted, powerful emotions continued to boil up inside her. She wanted to kiss the severity from his expression. Wanted to melt his ice. To muss his hair, to untie the perfect knot of his neck cloth. To chase the shadows from his eyes.

She laid her hand on his cheek, feeling unaccountably bold. She remained that way for a moment, the warmth of him, so alive and vital, beneath her palm. "You're a very persistent man."

"One of my many faults," he said. "I also prefer to read my

newspaper at the breakfast table uninterrupted, I dislike most people, I'm inordinately fond of my hound, and according to my sister, I'm a colossal bore."

Once again, he took her by surprise. He had a dog? She had always adored pups. It had broken her heart when her beloved Pomeranian Lou Lou had died last year. Surely a man who loved his dog couldn't be all ice and stone.

"Lightheartedness from you, my lord?" she teased. "You shock me."

"I could shock you more," he said, unsmiling.

She wondered what he meant. But it ceased to matter in the next moment, because the door to the sitting room pushed open behind them, followed by a piercing feminine shriek of indignation and punctuated with a thump as the dowager Marchioness of Featherstone fell to the floor in a dead swoon.

CHAPTER 4

"*I* simply cannot believe you're marrying Miss Lucy Chartrand. It's almost too ironic to be true," his sister said as the train carrying them back to London lumbered over its tracks.

Bette, in true fashion, was delighted by her brother's ignoble fall from grace. His indecorous tableau in the sitting room with Miss Chartrand had become the talk of the house party. It hadn't been his intention to entrap his future wife into a union. He'd wanted to persuade her. But the horrified wail Lady Featherstone had emitted upon finding them locked in a passionate embrace, followed by her fit of the vapors, had rather left the two of them without choice. Mrs. William Chartrand had been one of the first guests to race over the threshold, and the satisfied delight on that cunning woman's face had been undeniable.

Gareth sighed. "There is irony in it, indeed."

"You warned me away from her," his sister continued, wagging a finger at him like a governess admonishing her recalcitrant charge. "You said she was a dreadful influence."

"Unsuitable," he corrected grimly. "And then you told her so."

"Oh my. You two *have* been spending time together, haven't you?" Bette chuckled. "I never would have thought it of you, Gar. You always seem so proper and staid, and I haven't seen you take an interest in any lady, ever."

His sister's pet name for him rankled as it always did. He allowed it because he loved her more than any other person in the world. Even more than his pug, Hercules. They were the only surviving siblings, and both their parents had been gone for several years now. They remained all each other had in the world.

It was his greatest wish to see her settled and happy with a good husband who treated her well, to spoil his nieces and nephews to the point of ridiculousness. That had been the reason for attending this blasted house party. Bette had wanted to join the Lady's Suffrage Society. Gareth had known there would be a quantity of suitable gentlemen in attendance. However, he'd failed to imagine he would be the one to find himself leaving the house party decidedly attached.

"Apparently, I still possess the capacity to surprise and disappoint," he said. "Quite a relief since I'd begun to fear I'd lost my touch."

"You've never disappointed me, brother," Bette said, sympathy in her voice.

His sister knew the hell he'd been through with Anthea. Bette was younger by eight years, and he was desperately protective of her, but she'd been old enough to understand the misery that had been his daily existence.

"I'm relieved to hear it," he said.

"Are you in love with Miss Chartrand?" she asked suddenly.

Gareth nearly swallowed his tongue. "Of course not, Bette. Why would you ask such a thing?"

"Well, you were caught in a compromising position with her, and you've been spending time with her in private. I would imagine you must be harboring a secret *tendre*."

His ears went hot, a prickling feeling of shame settling in. "Unfortunately, love often has nothing to do with such matters. But that's hardly a topic for an innocent young lady."

"I'm not a little girl any longer, Gar," Bette told him quietly.

As if he required reminding. She was six-and-twenty. Older than he'd been when he had married Anthea. When he had been young and naïve and so damned foolish.

"I'm more than aware, but that doesn't change my opinion. I'll not further elaborate on my feelings for Miss Chartrand."

"But you do like her, at least, do you not?" his sister asked hopefully. "After how wretched you were with Anthea, I'd hate for you to find yourself similarly mired."

Wretched was hardly an apt descriptor. He'd been so unhappy that there had been a time when he had attempted to soothe his inner wounds with anything he could. Often, it had been wine or brandy or whatever spirit had been at hand. Until he'd realized he was hardly any better than his wife, whose dependency on laudanum had grown to impossible levels over the course of their marriage.

He cleared his throat, banishing thoughts of the past. "I like Miss Chartrand well enough, Bette. I'm afraid I can't hope for anything more than mild tolerance. But you needn't fear I'll be miserable. I very much doubt anyone could make me as unhappy as my dear, departed wife did."

He said the last with bitterness—old wounds possessed a tendency to fester. His had yet to entirely heal, despite the handful of years that had passed since Anthea's death.

"That's hardly a recommendation," Bette said, frowning. "I was hoping you'd tell me something terribly romantic, like you had fallen in love with Miss Chartrand at first sight and you knew that your souls were meant to join as one."

"What manner of drivel have you been reading, sister?" he asked. "I'm sorry to disillusion you. Romantic love is a futile notion. Belief in it will only lead to misery when the truth inevitably makes itself known."

"Oh, Gar." Bette reached for him, taking his hand in hers and giving it a squeeze. "I do so wish you had never married her. She brought you nothing but sorrow."

"I can assure you my regrets far surpass yours. But enough of the past. I'm afraid I have a wedding to arrange."

A vast wedding, apparently. Miss Chartrand's mother had already begun making plans. It would be an elaborate affair if she had anything to say about it. Miss Chartrand had been pale and grim as her mother had excitedly begun talking about having a gown commissioned in Paris and which flowers might best suit the grand occasion.

My dear girl, Mrs. Chartrand had said, grinning like a cat who had just slain a defenseless mouse, *you're marrying an earl.*

And that had been all the woman had cared about. Not the fact that he'd thoroughly dishonored her daughter by unleashing his carnal urges in plain view of one of the most pernicious gossips in polite society. Not her own daughter's distress, the pinched expression on her face, the plain fact that Miss Chartrand herself had no desire to wed.

But then, Gareth reckoned he was little better. Perhaps he should have told his conscience to go to the devil and left her alone. She'd been right. No one would have known about their moonlit indiscretion. They could have easily forgotten it had ever happened.

Except, he had known he wouldn't be able to. There was

something about the brash American heiress that both called to him and horrified him, all at the same time. He desired her in an innate way he'd never felt for another woman before. His every amorous encounter after Anthea's death had been a discreet, tempered affair. Lovers who received and took pleasure, who wanted the same physical intimacy he had yearned for in his marriage but had been denied, simply without the restricting bonds of emotion.

But Lucy Chartrand made him feel ravenous and wild. He wanted to devour her, debauch her, ask her for things he'd never dare demand of a respectable wife. And that was a hell of a thought to have whilst sitting with his sister, he thought grimly.

Bette was happily unaware of his mind's feverish imaginings. Instead, she was happily prattling on about wedding preparations. She was apparently delighted at the prospect of a new sister and very much looking forward to helping the Chartrand ladies in the planning of the wedding.

"Are you happy, Gar?" she asked him suddenly, the only pause in her otherwise endless trail of excited wedding planning.

He smiled reassuringly at his sister and lied. "Of course I am, dearest."

She cocked her head at him, her mouth tightening, and he knew that she could see through his subterfuge.

But then, he hadn't been happy in years. What else would she expect? The train rumbled over its tracks, the distance between himself and Miss Lucy Chartrand and the unwanted, troublesome lust she inspired in him growing.

～

"A GOWN from the House of Worth. We'll go directly to Paris with as much haste as possible. I'll have Parsons manage the arrangements."

Married, Lucy thought numbly, staring out the window. She was to be married.

"Has the earl discussed when he might like to have the wedding?" Mother asked, continuing in her excited planning.

"Two months, I believe," she said woodenly.

"Two months is hardly sufficient time to plan the most important wedding of the century," her mother bemoaned in typical dramatic fashion.

Oh, dear heavens. She should have known her mother would be more concerned with a wedding and a trousseau and with her own ability to preside over the affair than Lucy's own feelings on the matter.

"Mother, I hardly think my marriage to Lord Rexingham would be considered the wedding of the century," Lucy cautioned grimly.

"Of course it will be," Mother countered. "You are a Chartrand, and his lordship is an earl. Oh, my dear daughter, I'm so proud of you. There was a time when you insisted on imperiling your reputation with all those dreadful scandals, and I feared you'd never make a fine match. But you've proven me wrong."

Ironically, she'd been attempting to prove her mother right, only her plan had gone hopelessly awry. She'd kissed the wrong man, created a scandal with an earl, and now she had to answer for it by sacrificing her future.

"I still don't want to get married," she warned her mother, thinking for a wild, fleeting moment that she might simply abscond to the Continent. Hide until any resulting gossip faded away.

But then she reminded herself that she hadn't a penny to her name. Her father held all the purse strings so tightly that the rest of them might as well have been his marionettes, dangling helplessly, doing his bidding. How would she survive without a dollar of her own?

"I'll not hear another word of such nonsense," her mother snapped sternly. "You will marry the earl. You must, after what has happened. There isn't any other choice, you know. Your poor dear papa, should he hear of what happened, will be in a fine fury."

Yes, her father would undoubtedly be shocked and horrified at his daughter's actions.

"It would be worse if he knew I'd intended to meet a footman instead of the earl," she couldn't resist pointing out, a bit of her flagging spirits returning to her.

"Hold your tongue, Lucy," Mother snapped in a rare show of fury, her cheeks sporting twin patches of red. "I'll not hear another word of the mischief you'd planned. Fortunately, the fates were smiling on you, and you've been blessed with a second chance. Do not throw it away. If you do anything to ruin your future with Rexingham, I'll have no choice but to tell your father all about your hoyden ways. He won't be pleased, I can tell you that."

"When is Father ever pleased?" she grumbled glumly and mostly to herself.

"Lucy Amelia Chartrand," her mother chastised, "you'll not dare to say another word against your father. Apologize at once."

William Chartrand was a wealthy and powerful man, and he knew it. He treated everyone in his circle—his family included—as if they were inferior. Nothing and no one stood in his way. Lucy's girlhood had been marked by his foul tempers and selfishness. He wasn't any more generous with his love than he was with his money, though he was certain to provide his family with the best of everything, so the rest of the world might see and admire it.

As a result, Lucy had never shared a particularly close or fond relationship with him. She adored her sister and brother, even if Father had essentially created Duncan in his own mold. Mother's devoted loyalty to Father was, at times, a source of great contention. As was her determination to see Lucy and Madeline married off to a lord or a duke.

"I'm sorry, Mother," she said with a heavy sigh, not liking to make the concession and yet knowing it would render the next few months easier.

"Will you not at least face me when you're speaking to me?" her mother demanded.

Lucy turned away from the window to find her mother hovering nearby, a rare expression of concern etched in her face. "Does this please you?"

"Lucy, I know this isn't what you wanted," her mother said, her tone gentling as she crossed the room in a rustle of elegant skirts. "However, I firmly believe it's what's best for you. This silly dream of yours of starting your own cosmetics company simply wasn't meant to be. You have no need for money of your own. You're a Chartrand. And now, you'll be a countess as well."

It was another old argument. Lucy had been crafting her own creams for years. It had begun as a pastime to keep her occupied and had slowly grown into a very real desire for her own business. She hadn't wanted to spend her life known as William Chartrand's daughter. She had wanted to forge something for herself, to build her own empire. As a woman, she knew it wouldn't have been easy. And now, as a countess, it would likely prove impossible.

"It was never a silly dream to me," she said sadly.

"When you have a husband and family of your own, you'll see how wrong you were," her mother said, patting her arm fondly. "You're a woman now, and you haven't time to waste chasing girlish fancies. You'll be far happier as a wife and a countess. You'll have all the world at your fingertips."

It wasn't all the world Lucy wanted at her fingertips. Nor had it ever been. All she'd wanted was something for herself. But in the end, she had been the architect of her own ruin, and here she stood in a Yorkshire country house guest chamber, with only herself to blame.

She forced a smile she didn't feel. "I'm sure you're right, Mother."

Her mother gave her arm a squeeze. "I always am, dear."

"I MUST SAY that when I had the notion for this house party first in mind, I couldn't have predicted that it would lead to betrothals," Vivi, the Duchess of Bradford, said from her chair by the fireplace in her sitting room. "My original intention was to gather like minds and increase the membership and reach of the Lady's Suffrage Society."

"And you've done that as well," said Lady Clementine Hammond from her perch on a nearby window seat.

Clementine had become engaged to the Marquess of Dorset during the house party. While their betrothal had initially been the result of a scandalous situation, the couple had grown closer in recent days. Lucy was sure Clementine had fallen in love with the marquess, and if the way Dorset looked at his betrothed was any indication, the feeling was mutual.

"I'm very pleased that you've all decided to join us," Vivi said, but her countenance was clouded as she met Lucy's gaze across the sea of feminine faces gathered in the cheerful sitting room. "However, I am quite surprised. I didn't think you were particularly marriage-minded, Lucy."

Unfortunately, Lucy had been scandal-minded. And that

was how she'd mired herself in this wretched mess of her own making. She'd also conveyed her dearest hopes of starting her own cosmetics business with her friends, having shared some of her creams with them.

She forced a smile, however, not wanting her kind hostess and dear friend to know a moment of guilt. The fault for what had happened hadn't been Vivi's at all.

"Lord Rexingham has persuaded me to see the error of my ways," she said politely.

"Persuasion? Is that what you're calling it?" Madeline teased her.

She pinned her sister with a narrow-eyed glare. "Yes, dearest. It is."

It wasn't that Lucy didn't trust the ladies gathered. Her four friends—Vivi, Clementine, Lady Edith Smythe, and Lady Charity Manners—were loyal and wonderful friends she was grateful to have made during her time in England. And of course, she would trust her sister with her own life.

However, she didn't think she could speak about what had occurred between herself and the earl in the gardens without being beset by embarrassment. Her behavior had been terribly forward, even by her own standards, which were admittedly lax.

"Did the earl catch a bee in your skirts?" Lady Charity asked cheekily, referencing the now-infamous incident that had led to Clementine's engagement to Lord Dorset.

"Thankfully not," she managed, her smile weakening.

Far worse. The only thing up her skirts had been his hand. And the memory of his touch skimming along her most intimate flesh made an unwanted ache pulse to life deep in her core. Good heavens, what was wrong with her? It would seem that not even the prospect of a looming, unwanted marriage had a dousing effect on the fires of longing raging inside her where the Earl of Rexingham was concerned.

"Sometimes, the appropriate stimulus is all that is required to change one's mind," Edith said. "The breeding habits of sheep, for instance, suggest—"

"Oh, Edith," Charity interrupted. "Pray don't tell us about sheep mating again. I'll never be able to look at a lamb in the same way again as it is."

"It couldn't have been as bad as when she tried to expound on the vagaries of whale dung," Madeline added with a delicate shudder.

Edith was the most intelligent woman Lucy had ever met. She devoured scientific treatises as if they were sheer poetry. She knew something about everything, including the scents used in the making of her extensive perfume collection.

"But I've already told you that ambergris isn't specifically whale dung," Edith argued, frowning from where she was seated on a divan, a book in her lap, her brilliant red hair shining bright in the sunlight cascading through the window at her back. "It's a substance found within the feces of the Physeter Macrocephalus."

"You can try to explain it to us in every language you know, my dear, but I'm afraid it won't help your case," Charity said gently. "Let's play a favorite game of mine called Pretend It Never Happened and carry on with our conversation."

"What were we talking about?" Clementine asked with a frown.

"Lucy's marriage, of course," Madeline chimed in cheerfully, grinning at Lucy in despicable fashion that suggested she was enjoying her sister's discomfiture, the minx.

Lucy drummed her fingers on the armrests of her chair. "I'd prefer it if we wouldn't, truly. It's months away, and I don't want to think about it any more than necessary.

Mother has already given me a headache by making an endless number of plans concerning my trousseau and dress. I had to listen to her drone on about Brussels lace and myrtle flowers for an entire hour."

"That truly sounds wretched," Charity commiserated. "Given the choice between listening to a discussion on lace and flowers or sheep mating, I'm afraid I'd have to endure the sheep mating."

"The crossbreeding of sheep is quite interesting," Edith insisted. "I've read a great deal about it."

"Of course you have, dear," Charity said, patting Edith's arm in consoling fashion. "And you know I adore you, but I'll never quite understand your affection for certain subjects."

"Such as diseases of the throat," Lucy couldn't help but to add, thinking of the book she'd found in Edith's room during a previous meeting of their little coterie. "What was that word I'd never heard before that I read in one of your medical books, Edith? I've already forgotten it, and I did so want to use it in a conversation one day just to see if I could befuddle the person I was speaking with. Pult-something. Pultmaceous? No, that's not right. Pultcraceous?"

"Pultaceous," Edith corrected.

"That's it," Lucy said, then bit her lip. "I'll likely forget it again. Perhaps you should write it down for me."

"I fear it won't have the intended effect when you have to extract a paper from somewhere on your person and read it, sister," Madeline drawled.

"I'll simply have to use it in a letter instead, then," Lucy said, relieved at the silly diversion and the chance to avoid thinking about her looming nuptials.

"You can write it in a letter to the earl since he's left the house party with such haste," Charity suggested. "Why did he leave so quickly?"

"I don't know," Lucy admitted.

She hadn't realized he was leaving until after she'd escaped from her mother's endless wedding chatter, and by then, he'd already been packed away in a carriage that was disappearing down the meandering Sherborne Manor approach. He'd left her a note that had been alarmingly succinct.

Miss Chartrand—
It is in the best interest of us both that I return to London
forthwith.
Yours,
Rexingham

He hadn't even bothered to explain, to say goodbye, to make further plans. But then, they'd already proven themselves rather incapable of restraint. Perhaps he hadn't trusted himself to remain, lest he fully compromise her.

"He's probably running from Mother," Madeline said wryly. "And who can blame him? She had the poor man cornered for the better part of an hour this morning. Maybe if you're fortunate, Lucy, he'll book passage on the first available ship and sail away and hide."

Lucy knew better. The earl had been determined. His honor refused to accept anything less than a marriage between them. And now, she would have no choice but to marry him and abandon her dreams of owning her own business. There was the possibility she could cry off, but she didn't fool herself. Her mother may have been tolerant of her past foibles, but Lucy had never been caught in such a compromising position so publicly before.

"I'm afraid his sense of honor won't accept anything less than marriage," Lucy said.

Vivi's gaze was searching. "Do you want to marry him?

Because I'm certain if we applied enough pressure to Lady Featherstone, she would hold her tongue. Apologies, Edith."

Lady Featherstone was Edith's mother, but their friend was more than aware of her gossip-loving mother's reputation and her unabashedly wagging tongue.

"You needn't apologize," Edith said. "I understand that *Maman* is not universally adored, and for good reason. Lucy, if you want me to speak to my mother on your behalf, I'm more than happy to do so."

"There's no need," Lucy reassured her friend, though the temptation was there.

If the Marchioness of Featherstone promised to keep what she'd seen a secret, then perhaps there wouldn't be any need for Lucy to marry the Earl of Rexingham. But no, the damage had been done. And by now, the rest of the house party was more than aware that something had occurred.

Something untoward, followed by an engagement announcement. Word traveled fast at country house parties. Lucy hadn't realized just how quickly gossip could burn through a small gathering. But then, New York City society was no better. She ought not to have been surprised. The bucolic scenery was different, but people—wherever they were—remained steadfastly the same.

"Are you sure?" Edith asked gently, her blue eyes earnest behind her spectacles.

"I appreciate the offer, but at this point, my mother has likely leapt onto the roof to make the announcements," she said. "The earl and I suit quite well."

In one sense. A furious flush climbed up her throat at the thought. She hoped none of her friends would notice.

"You're blushing, dearest," Madeline said, dashing the hope in true sisterly fashion.

"You don't have any mercy, do you?" she grumbled.

"Some, dearest," her sister said. "But I reserve that for

truly deserving occasions. I'm afraid you've managed to find yourself in this betrothal through your own machinations."

"Machinations?" Charity asked, perking up in her chair with undisguised interest. "Do tell us what happened. I sensed there was something far more than what you've said so far."

Lucy cast a glare in her sister's direction before turning back to Charity. "As my dear sister suggested, I'm at fault for this entire affair. I was intending to meet someone in the gardens, but the man I ended up meeting instead was the earl."

"It wasn't Viscount Wilton you were meeting in the gardens, was it?" Charity asked quickly.

Far too quickly.

Was there something between her bold friend and the staid, awkward viscount who had a penchant for telling jokes? Interesting. Lucy hadn't taken note of it before, but there was a decidedly sharp edge of interest in Charity's voice.

"No, it wasn't," she told her friend. "Would it have concerned you if it had been?"

Charity smiled brightly. "Of course not. Why would it? Wilton is a deadly bore. I merely would have been surprised. And indeed, with the way the unattached men at this house party have been pairing up with ladies, he was a natural guess. There aren't many remaining."

An excellent point, but Lucy was certain there was more to it than that. Charity was protesting far too much.

"It wasn't Lord Wilton," she said again. "It doesn't truly matter who it was, for he didn't appear anyway."

There was no sense in getting poor Robert sacked from his position as footman. He'd certainly demonstrated better judgment than she had in having second thoughts about their assignation.

And Madeline was right. This mess was her own making. She'd gone to the gardens, she'd kissed the Earl of Rexingham, and then she'd done far more. Not just that night but the next morning as well. There was no excuse for her behavior, no one else she could blame.

Well, except for the earl himself. But that was another matter entirely.

"So you intended to meet an unattached gentleman in the gardens," Clementine said. "But then the earl appeared instead?"

"Yes, the earl appeared instead, and I mistook him for the other gentleman, and, well, I'm afraid I quite lost my head." She gave a sheepish smile to her friends. "I'm happy to report that the Earl of Rexingham decidedly does not kiss like a fish."

Edith's face flamed at the reference to one of their recent conversations about her past suitor, Mr. George Brougham, who apparently hadn't been nearly as talented at kissing as her current amour, the rakish and dashing Mr. Valentine Blakemoor.

"I'm relieved to hear it," Edith told her solemnly. "No one ought to suffer such appallingly wet and sloppy attempts. When a gentleman knows how to kiss properly, it's the most glorious thing. I'm glad I didn't realize the difference until I was firmly on the shelf. Otherwise, I can't begin to imagine the scandals I would have caused. Poor *Maman* would have been swooning all over the ballrooms of London."

The ladies all chuckled at the thought of Edith, who'd arrived at the house party a shy wallflower and had blossomed into a woman who had finally defied her managing mother, kissing her way through London.

"I would have dearly liked to see Lady Featherstone swooning this morning," Charity said. "It must have been quite a sight. Pray don't take offense, Edith dear. It's just that your mother spread that dreadful rumor about me posing as naked as a babe for that Venus painting, and I've never forgiven her for it."

Everyone knew about the infamous Venus painting and Charity supposedly having sat for the portrait. The rumor was so salacious that it had even crossed the Atlantic and reached New York City's high society.

"I know, Charity, and I'm so sorry," Edith said. "I've asked her never to repeat it."

"And I love you for your loyalty, dear friend." Charity smiled, though it was strained, for her reputation had been rather tarnished by the scandal. "Fortunately, I don't have to worry about gossip and being proper. I have no intention of ever marrying."

"Never, my dear?" Vivi asked, her brow furrowed. "Are you certain?"

Charity shuddered. "I've never been more certain of anything in my life."

Lucy held her tongue and refrained from reminding her friend she'd once felt the same.

CHAPTER 5

TWO MONTHS LATER

*I*t had indeed been the wedding of the century.

Thanks to Mother, who had orchestrated every detail, down to the number of diamonds in the tiara Lucy had worn in her hair and the types of flowers adorning the five-foot-tall wedding cake that had taken almost two months to construct. And thanks to Father's largesse, of course. Mr. William Chartrand had very loudly declared to everyone within earshot at the ceremony and ensuing wedding breakfast that his daughter was a countess now and that no expense had been spared to mark the festive occasion of her nuptials to the Earl of Rexingham.

Now, at long last, the carriage was quiet, the hundreds of guests who had joined them for the wedding and celebration no longer surrounding them. Lucy was alone with her husband, a man she'd scarcely seen for more than the span of a quarter hour at a time over the last few weeks of preparation. A man who had taken great care to maintain a proper distance, to never linger in her presence alone since the disastrous scandal they'd created at Sherborne Manor.

A man who had spoken fewer than five sentences to her since they had officially become husband and wife.

She was tired, her feet ached, her head ached from the tightness of her coiffure and the heaviness of her tiara. Her face ached from all the feigned smiles she'd kept firmly pinned to her lips for the duration of the nuptials. And her heart ached at the final, irrefutable proof that her dream of starting her own cosmetics business would never be realized.

"You are quiet, Lady Rexingham," her new husband observed from the opposite side of the resplendent carriage they shared—more proof that the earl hadn't been after her massive dowry, just like the marriage contract he had signed honoring his commitment to her keeping control over her own funds.

"I'm weary," she said simply.

"You wear the somber mien of a woman attending her own funeral," he quipped, unsmiling himself and so unfairly handsome that a part of her couldn't help but be moved by the sight of him.

What did he expect her to say?

She hadn't wanted a husband.

Hadn't wanted to marry anyone, let alone him. Two months hadn't changed her opinion on the matter, and neither had her Worth gown and Brussels lace and the thousands of pounds in flowers that had festooned the church.

"Perhaps in some ways, I am," she said finally. "Certainly, this is the death of my life as I knew it."

"But the beginning of another part of the journey."

She inclined her head. "As you say, my lord."

"I do wish you might call me Gareth." Despite his words, the earl's tone was frosty.

He was so very aloof, his jaw held at a rigid angle that made her wonder if he had been carved from marble instead of made from flesh and bone.

"And I do wish you might call me Lucy instead of Lady Rexingham," she countered peevishly, "for that is my name."

"Your name is also now Lady Rexingham, my dear," he said curtly. "You may as well resign yourself to it. I must thank you for not weeping during the ceremony or the wedding breakfast, but no one who looked upon you would have mistaken you for a happy bride."

The last comment was particularly harsh.

She laced her hands together tightly in her lap, regarding him solemnly. "You know that I didn't want to marry."

"You might have cried off at any moment during these last two months," he pointed out wryly.

"Surely you know I couldn't have done so. Not when my mother had begun such lavish plans for our wedding and the newspapers here in London and back home in New York City were reporting on it. To say nothing of the manner in which Lady Featherstone caught us in a terribly compromising position at Sherborne Manor."

The mention of their torrid embrace sent heat flaring deep inside her. She hadn't forgotten the way the earl had made her feel. Hadn't forgotten how his kisses and wicked caresses had so thoroughly brought her to life.

"I exercised a shocking lack of restraint," he said coolly. "Let it not be forgotten the manner in which our original scandal began, however. We wouldn't have found ourselves here together in this carriage and in this marriage if you hadn't mistaken me for someone else and thrown yourself in my arms in the gardens that night."

The reminder of her folly had her cheeks going hot. But she wasn't going to allow him to make her wilt beneath the intensity of his scrutiny. They were married now. Husband and wife. What a foreign, almost unbelievable notion. This man was hers, and she was his.

It was terrifying.

"I do think you're every bit as culpable as I am, my lord," she said pointedly. "I may have kissed you, but you kissed me back."

"I succumbed to my weaker, base impulses." His blue stare flicked over her, assessing. "I'll endeavor not to allow it to happen again."

Was he suggesting he found fault with her? Lucy didn't dabble in vanity, but she was more than aware of her appearance. Specifically, in the wedding gown she still wore, every detail carefully chosen to accentuate her figure in all the best ways. She knew the effect she had on men as well. And she would be willing to wager her diamond tiara that Rexingham was not unmoved.

She managed a small smile, trying to cover her hurt at his frigid demeanor. "How relieved I am to hear it, sir."

The carriage ride descended into a miserable silence.

Frustrated, Lucy turned to look out the window at the passing scenery, London at once familiar and yet entirely changed. How odd to think of it as her home now, to know that she would never again return to her father's mansion in New York City for anything other than a visit. Thank heavens she had her friends and Madeline here and the Lady's Suffrage Society. Without them, she'd be as lost as a dinghy hopelessly adrift in the sea.

"When we arrive, the domestics will greet us for a formal introduction," he said, jolting her from her thoughts.

Her head swung back to him, as elegant and immovable as he'd been from the moment she'd first seen him at the altar that morning. Their wedding breakfast had been held at the massive town house Mother had leased for their sojourn in London society. Now, it was late afternoon, approaching evening, and they were traveling to Rexingham's St James abode, which she'd only visited on one previous occasion.

"How kind of you to arrange it," she offered politely, her stomach tightening into a knot of dread.

Was she ready to take on the responsibility of being a countess? Of being this icy stranger's wife? She was sure she was destined to failure. She could have been happy with her cosmetics business, living above a shop somewhere back home in New York or perhaps even in Paris, controlling her own future. But now, that dream had slipped forever through her fingers. She had gone from the expectations her parents had settled upon her to the expectations her new husband would.

"My housekeeper, Mrs. Parr, suggested it," Rexingham said smoothly. "I had quite forgotten having done so for my first marriage as well."

The mentioning of his previous wife nettled Lucy. She couldn't deny it. The woman seemed a specter determined to haunt her.

She buried her fingers in the voluminous fall of her skirts so he wouldn't see them clenching. "How kind of Mrs. Parr, then."

He drummed his fingers on his thigh, looking bored and disinterested. "I'm not sure kindness is involved. Practicality is more apt. You'll be overseeing the servants. They may as well know who you are, and likewise, you may as well see their faces. It's standard practice in large households."

Standard practice. Of course. Naturally, there was nothing special about her presence in his household. Nor about their union itself. If she'd had any doubt about that, she only needed to look at her husband's impassive countenance to recollect it. He was not any more pleased to have her as his wife than she was to be his countess. It was a match made in misery.

And lust.

But even lust was far preferable to the indifference he

emanated now. She'd liked him better when his lips were on hers and his hand had been under her skirts.

"Will Bette be joining us?" she asked politely instead of addressing his somewhat insulting explanation.

It had belatedly occurred to her that his sister had been left behind at the wedding breakfast with the rest of the dwindling throng of revelers.

"Naturally," the earl said smoothly. "Claremont House is where she lives."

Ah, yes. Lucy had nearly forgotten that Rexingham's London residence possessed its own grand title and rambling presence. It was fitting that even his home would be arrogant and supercilious.

But Lucy kept that to herself.

Instead, she smiled. "How nice. It will be lovely to have her for company."

Because it was more than apparent that her new husband didn't appear interested in keeping her company. Indeed, he rather looked as if he considered throwing himself from the moving carriage a preferable fate to continuing their stilted conversation.

"I trust you won't be instructing my impressionable sister in the finer art of creating a scandal," he said, his tone steeped in warning.

And she wanted to punch him in his aristocratic, haughty nose.

She didn't, however.

She gritted her teeth. "I'm sure I don't know what you're speaking of, my lord."

"No? I can't fathom that your memory is so short, my dear. Since the happy occasion of our betrothal, I've been besieged by tales of the scandals you've created, both in New York City and abroad."

Guilt mingled with outrage. Had he been investigating

her as if she were some manner of common criminal? Had he been so horrified at the prospect of forever aligning himself with a dreadful American that he'd hired a Pinkerton?

"Are you saying you've been spying on me, my lord?"

"I wouldn't call it that. Merely better acquainting myself with my bride."

"And yet, you've spent so little time in my presence over the last two months," she couldn't resist pointing out, her smarting pride making her tongue far too loose.

She didn't want him to see how much his lack of attention in her had affected her. And heavens, why should she care? She hadn't wanted this marriage. Didn't want to be a wife. *His* wife.

"I didn't realize you'd missed me, my dear."

His tone, like his words, was hideously polite. Unflappable. Did nothing bother him? Where was the passionate man who had so thoroughly seduced her in the garden, in the library, in the sitting room? She longed to rail at him, to shout, to throw herself across the carriage, into his lap, and kiss that forbidding line from his lips.

"Don't be silly," she said, striving for a suitably breezy tone, as if she were as imperturbable as he appeared to be. "I didn't miss you at all. I was far too busy attending to other matters."

He was silent for a moment, and she was intensely aware of his regard. Studying her. Leaving her skin tingling with heat. His gaze was as intimate as a touch.

"What matters?" he asked, his voice silken.

Almost dangerous.

She wondered what he would do if she lied and told him she'd been kissing as many gentlemen as she could while she was still unattached. The temptation was there, burning like a hot coal in her belly. But before she could act on it, the carriage slowed to a halt. They had arrived at Claremont House.

Her new life had officially begun.

ALONE AT LAST, in the private confines of his study, Gareth poured himself far too much brandy and sat in an over-stuffed leather chair, staring unseeing into the dying embers of the evening fire. His faithful pug, Hercules, was curled up on a nearby cushion, gently snoring, worn out by the excitement of meeting Lucy.

The day had been, in a word, torturous.

Much like the two months that had preceded it. Gareth had spent the time between his wayward actions at Sherborne Manor and his wedding to Miss Lucy Chartrand in a state of preparation. Every hint of Anthea had been removed from his homes. Wall coverings, furniture, even the Axminster and lingering pictures he'd been too distracted to notice had been taken away.

The countess's apartments, which had been closed up for several years, had been opened and aired. Thank God for Bette, who had spared him the effort of having to make decisions over the new wall coverings and paint, the new bed and pictures adorning the walls. He didn't have the slightest inclination of what a woman would want her bedroom to look like.

Not just any woman. Lucy. His American firebrand who had been charming men on both sides of the Atlantic, leaving a string of brokenhearted suitors in her wake. Christ, what had he been thinking, offering for her? Twelve years had passed between his first doomed wedding and his second, and it would seem he hadn't grown a whit more intelligent in all that time. He was still foolish, making mistakes, still choosing the wrong bride for all the wrong reasons.

He lifted his glass of brandy to his lips, cursing himself, and drained half its contents in one burning gulp.

A faint tap on the door roused him from his self-imposed stupor. Hercules raised his head, the sound jolting him from sleep but not troubling him enough to go investigate. For a moment, Gareth's pulse leapt. What if it was Lucy? They had parted ways after the formal dinner they'd shared with Bette, his new wife adjourning to her bedchamber alone. He'd been relieved and disappointed.

Relieved because he wasn't sure he could trust himself not to ravish her like a ravening lunatic tonight. And disappointed because he had been hoping she might want him to join her. Instead, she'd been impersonal and polite, excusing herself from the dining room and hastening to her private apartments. Gareth had retreated to the room that had been his haven during his failed marriage to Anthea.

Likely, it would prove a haven again in this disastrous union.

"Come," he called reluctantly, hoping it wasn't Lucy.

Hoping it *was* her, too.

The door opened, revealing his sister, who hovered at the threshold wearing an expression he'd seen far too often.

Concern.

"May I join you, brother?" she asked softly.

He rose in deference to her, lifting his glass in mock salute. "Only if you promise not to take offense at my mood, dearest."

Hercules lifted his head, looked at Bette, and then snuggled back into his cushion with a dog noise of contentment.

She slipped inside, closing the door softly at her back and moving across the chamber in slipper-shod feet. "Your mood should be a happy one today. It was your wedding day."

Gareth took another fortifying sip of brandy. "I'm afraid matrimony is a familiar, if not comfortable, state for me."

"That's entirely understandable, given what happened with Anthea." Bette frowned, studying him in that sisterly way she had, which always seemed to slice through to the heart of him. "But you must realize that Lucy is nothing at all like Anthea was."

"Of course she isn't like Anthea." He settled his brandy on a nearby table, knowing it was poor form to be swilling the stuff before his sister. "But Miss Chartrand is still hardly the sort of woman I would have wished for as my wife."

She was bold. Brash. Passionate. Scandalous.

And the sight of her in her ethereal wedding gown today, a sylph gliding toward him down the aisle, a gorgeous, desirable goddess who tempted him far more than he found comfortable or practical, had been almost enough to send him to his knees before hundreds of guests. It had been a moment of sheer terror combined with violent, unadulterated desire. He still didn't know what to make of it or her. Nor to his reaction to her.

He had hoped that the intervening weeks would have lessened or even quelled his need for her. But his body had been decisive on the matter. They had not. He'd spent the entirety of their interminable carriage ride back to Claremont House in the fierce grip of a lust so potent, it had been all he could do to keep from reaching across the carriage, hauling her into his lap, and having his wicked way with her. He'd retreated behind a wall of ice instead, not trusting himself.

"Why not, Gar?" Bette asked softly. "I like Lucy a great deal."

As did he. But not in a way that was appropriate to admit to his innocent sister.

Gareth cleared his throat and busied himself with turning

away and taking up a fire poker, stirring up the coals in the hearth. "I'm relieved you find her unobjectionable. However, I must remind you that she's not exactly a paragon. Certainly, she harbors a great deal of scandals in her past, none of which are worthy of repeating to you. Suffice it to say, she has made her fair share of errors in judgment."

And by errors in judgment, he meant men.

Countless men she'd charmed and kissed and done God knew what with. He didn't want to think about that. Didn't want to think about anyone who had come before him. And the notion of anyone coming after him…no. He couldn't countenance it just now.

"But there is a warmth to her that is so often lacking," Bette protested, joining him by the fire. "I see the way she looked at you when she thought no one was looking today, and I'm convinced she's quite smitten with you."

Lucy? Smitten with him? Ha! His American spitfire had any number of men falling at her feet. Servants, lords, wealthy railroad barons, department store owners, the list of her conquests was unending. Finally, he'd forced himself to cease digging.

"Perhaps she was holding in a sneeze," he suggested mildly, giving the coals another unnecessary stir.

Bette chuckled. "You're far too modest, brother dear. You're considered an excellent catch."

"Despite my dead wife and the rumors that I drove her to her untimely demise, you mean?" he asked, unable to keep the acid from his voice.

"Yes, despite that," his sister said firmly. "You can't continue to allow Anthea to destroy you from the grave, you know. Lucy is your wife now."

God.

She was. What the hell had he done? he wondered bleakly, returning the fire poker to its stand.

"I'm well aware that today was my wedding day," he told Bette firmly. "I don't need you to remind me, Bette."

"It seems you do need me," his sister countered archly. "Else why would you be lingering here in your study, drinking brandy alone, leaving your new wife abandoned upstairs when you ought to be with her, enjoying your wedding night?"

His ears went hot.

He pinned Bette with a narrow-eyed glare. "You aren't to know of such matters."

"Such matters as the consummation of a marriage? Don't be silly, Gar. I'm a woman fully grown. Of course I know about it."

He swallowed against a rising knot in his throat, his neck cloth suddenly too damned tight. "How do you know? Miss Chartrand didn't tell you, did she?"

"No, she didn't," Bette reassured him tartly, "and you had best think of her as Lady Rexingham now. She's no longer Miss Chartrand, is she?"

"Then who?" he demanded, wondering if he had to challenge some villain to a duel or have a sharp word with one of her friends' mamas.

"Aunt Regina, if you must know," Bette relented. "She's taken me under her wing for such talks at your request, if you'll recall."

Christ, yes. He had asked their mother's sister to be the family member to whom Bette deferred in all matters feminine. He hadn't given a thought as to what those entailed at the time.

He wasn't certain he wanted to think about them now, either.

"Of course," he managed gruffly. "I'm grateful to Aunt Regina for…providing the necessary edification."

His sister chuckled, plainly amused at his expense. "Gar, are you flushing?"

The skin on his neck prickled, and his face had indeed taken on a hotness that had nothing to do with the dying fire he'd been prodding back to life.

He glowered at Bette. "Naturally not. Gentlemen don't flush."

"Hmm," she murmured, a noncommittal sound that suggested she didn't believe him.

"Shouldn't you be abed by now, Bette?" he snapped, irritated with his sister for her meddling.

For seeing through him, for knowing him too well.

And irritated with himself for his maddening inability to control his own emotions and reactions. It was another fault he would lay at the door of his unwanted bride. He was never this affected. She was to blame.

"I daresay I should, but I was worrying about my beloved brother hiding in his study and being a horse's arse to his new bride," Bette said, shocking him with her frank language.

"Where did you learn such a crude phrase?" he demanded. "And if you say Aunt Regina, I'm clearly going to have to have a talk with her."

His sister gave him a secretive smile. "It wasn't Aunt Regina."

By God.

"Who was it?" he demanded.

The smile deepened, mischief glittering in her blue eyes, so like his own. "Perhaps I'll tell you another day if you go and tend to your bride."

"You'll tell me now," he growled. "A gently bred young lady shouldn't be engaging in such vulgar speech."

"Some other day," Bette insisted. "Now, go to your wife."

She rose on her toes and pressed a sisterly kiss to his cheek. "All my love, brother dear."

With that, his wily sibling took her leave from the study, having neatly routed him. Gareth and Hercules watched her go.

CHAPTER 6

$\mathcal{T}$he knock on the door connecting Lucy's chamber to her new husband's jolted her from her thoughts. She'd been pacing the chamber, wondering when he would join her at last, and now, it would seem she finally had her answer. She'd sent her lady's maid away an hour or more ago, hoping her husband would materialize. Wanting to be alone with him. Needing a chance to shatter the icy politeness that had descended between them like an immovable curtain.

She went to the door, pulling it open herself, and found him standing there, impossibly tall and handsome, every inch the polished lord.

"Lord Rexingham," she greeted formally, still uncertain of where they stood.

Everything was new. As new as the furnishings and wall coverings and curtains in her chamber, all of which had proven a pleasant surprise. She rather suspected her husband hadn't been behind the recent improvements but that Bette had.

"My dear," he said politely, sketching an elegant bow as if

they were strangers facing each other in a ballroom instead of husband and wife on their wedding night. "I came to see if you had settled in to your chamber."

"I have," she said, taking a step in retreat so that he might enter her new domain. "I must thank you for the welcome. I hadn't expected to find the chamber so well suited to me."

He cleared his throat, his gaze unreadable. "Save your praise for Bette. This was all her hand."

She hadn't been wrong about that, then. The small barb of disappointment she felt was ridiculous, she knew. Likely, had the earl overseen the changes himself, he would have chosen all wrong. He was a man after all.

"I will thank her in the morning," she said simply.

He stared at her for a long, interminable moment, still hovering at the threshold as if he feared he might fall into a pit of hissing vipers should he take a step within. "Have you uttered the phrase *horse's arse* in the presence of my sister, by any chance?"

Of all the things Lucy might have expected her new husband to say, that hadn't been even close to the list.

"Of course not," she told him. "Why do you ask?"

He shook his head, sliding a long finger into his neck cloth as if to loosen it. "No reason."

What a strange man he was. "Would you care to join me?" she invited when he continued to hover in the doorway.

"Not tonight, I don't think," he said, stepping forward and bending to drop a chaste kiss on her cheek. "Good night, Lady Rexingham."

The graze of his lips against her skin brought unwanted heat sparking to life inside Lucy. But surely he didn't intend to avoid consummating their marriage. After those potent, passionate kisses they'd shared, those sinful embraces, the last thing she expected was for him to politely retreat.

"You are going to bed?" she asked, feeling suddenly nervous and uncertain of herself.

"The day has been a long one. I imagine you would like some rest."

How polite he was being. How reserved and removed. The detached air he'd been wearing as surely as his elegant wedding attire was still firmly in place. He moved to take his leave, and something inside her snapped.

"Wait."

The word left her sharply. Startling him. He turned to look at her.

She licked her lips, shyness threatening to overwhelm her. "Is it not customary for the bride and groom to spend the night of their wedding together?"

"I wasn't certain that was what you wished," he said politely, a grim, mocking half smile curling his lips. "My last bride spent her wedding night huddled in the bed, crying herself to sleep."

Was he trying to frighten her? Warn her?

Lucy couldn't be sure. There was so much about her new husband that remained an enigma. She'd had a moment of terrible clarity earlier during the seemingly endless ceremony that had unfolded before London's finest when she had realized it was possible she would never truly know him.

It had made a cold trill of unease slide down her spine. His eyes had been on hers, and for a moment, she'd thought he had read her thoughts. But then he had smiled in that jaded, aloof manner of his, and it had been meant to reassure her, although it had quite the opposite effect. And the ceremony had continued on.

"Why did she do so?" she asked now, wanting to understand something of his past, if not his present.

Perhaps it would help her to understand him.

"I disgusted her," he said, his simple response shocking her.

"What would she have possibly found in you to disgust her, my lord?" Lucy's gaze traveled over his tall, lean form, finding him impossibly attractive. "Do you have scales hiding underneath your shirt?"

His lips twitched, and for a moment, she thought he might give her a true smile. But then the sadness that never seemed far returned, and his mouth remained as it was, grim and joyless. "No scales. It was my desire to consummate the marriage that was the problem. She preferred a bottle of laudanum to the marriage bed."

Lucy began to comprehend some of the pain that seemed to linger beneath his outwardly polished surface. "I'm sorry, Gareth."

"You needn't waste your pity on me," he said. "I made peace with the past long ago."

It hardly seemed he had, for it to continue to haunt him so. What had his former wife done to render him so bitter?

"I don't pity you," she told him, raising her chin and telling herself that she must be bold in their interactions if she wanted this marriage of theirs to succeed. For suddenly, she very much did want it to flourish, despite the reticence with which she'd approached it. "Nor do I take issue with your desire to consummate our marriage. I welcome it."

He stilled, and the mask he wore so well slipped, revealing something of the true man hiding beneath the surface. "You welcome it?"

Her fingers went to the buttons on her bodice, and she held his stare, willing him to stay with her. To break the chains of the past. "I do."

A button came free, then another.

His icy blue gaze dipped, watching her progress. There was an undeniable flare of awareness, a subtle shift in the air. Three more buttons opened. He remained where he had been, standing halfway between her and the door between their bedrooms. Not leaving, but not joining her either. It was as if they were engaged in a silent battle, her willing him closer and him trying to slip away.

She didn't want him as an audience, she realized, but rather, as a participant.

"Will you assist?" she asked softly.

"Your lady's maid can see to it." His tone was cool.

Lucy decided not to be deterred. "I don't want her help. I want yours."

She moved to him, closing the separation, crossing the divide. It felt as if she traveled a great deal farther than the handful of paces it took her to reach him. He remained still and silent, watching her with a growing wariness, but also with an undeniable heated interest. She spun around, presenting him with her back.

"Will you help me to remove my train?"

The elaborate fall of fabric and silk roses over her bustle was cumbersome, but it was also fastened with hooks and eyes from behind. She knew she could slip out of it alone, but it would be easier if he helped.

She waited, all too aware of him at her back, wondering if he would deny her and leave after all, as he had planned. But then there was a subtle tug at her gown, a loosening, followed by the removal of the heavy weight of her train.

"Thank you," she murmured unsteadily, finding it strangely erotic to have him behind her, where she couldn't see him. Nothing but his presence at her back, crackling like live electric wires.

"Lucy," he said, his voice a low, velvet rasp in the quiet of the room.

"Yes?"

"If I help you to remove any other garment, I'm not certain I'll be able to maintain my restraint."

He said it so calmly, and yet his words of warning were laden with blatant sensual promise. Heat blossomed in her belly.

"What if I don't want you to be restrained?" she dared to ask softly.

He made a sound, part growl. "You're playing with fire, my dear."

Likely, she was. But it didn't matter. She wanted him. Longed for him. In the days spent preparing for their wedding, that had been the most astonishing discovery—despite her lack of desire for marriage, she very desperately did yearn for more of his kisses, his caresses. For more of everything. The completion she'd been denied.

"Perhaps I like the thrill of trying to keep from getting burned," she suggested, her back still presented to him, holding her breath.

Waiting.

He said nothing for a few moments, and then he stepped forward, and his mouth came down on her nape, a hot promise that made her gasp as desire and surprise arced through her. His hands settled on her waist in a possessive hold, anchoring her to him.

"I'm trying to be a gentleman this evening," he murmured, kissing the hollow behind her ear.

She shivered, and not from cold. There was no chance of a chill in the air this evening, not with him at her back, burning into her like the fire he'd likened himself to.

"I don't want you to be a gentleman. I want you to be my husband."

"The husband you didn't want," he reminded her, guiding her around so that she faced him, his countenance impassive. "I'll not press my advantage. I know you weren't desirous of

80

this union any more than I was. Perhaps some time to acquaint yourself with the notion is best."

He was wrong about that. She had spent these last, interminable weeks preparing for her wedding, resigning herself to her fate. And now she wanted the man who had kissed her with such passionate intensity in the gardens at Sherborne Manor. She wanted the man who had lifted her onto the window seat and kissed her breathless, the man who had put his mouth on her breasts in the dark night and made her feel exquisite sensations she'd never felt before.

"I've had ample time to do so while awaiting our nuptials," she reminded him, resuming the line of buttons. Her bodice gaped open. Every undergarment beneath had been chosen with great care and consideration for the evening of her wedding day.

"Lucy."

The way he said her name was itself a caress.

She loosened her skirt and shrugged her bodice to the floor. "Gareth."

His nostrils flared, the first sign that he was struggling to control himself. She dropped her skirts and stepped out of them, then reached for the tapes keeping her petticoat in place.

"Let me," he said, his fingers suddenly tangling with hers.

He'd lost the battle.

Lucy smiled and moved her hands away, allowing him to untie the knot. Her petticoats slid to the floor in a soft *shush* of sound. Her corset cover was next, and then she was standing before him in her red satin corset that she'd had commissioned as part of her trousseau, also from Paris.

"My God," he said, running his hand over the smooth fabric, following the line of stiff boning from her breasts to her waist.

"Will you help me take it off?" she asked.

He was watching the progress of his hands on her, following her curves, caressing her through the corset. She lowered her gaze to watch as well, enjoying the juxtaposition of his large, strong hands on her dainty corset trimmed with lace.

"Turn," he said.

She obeyed, spinning about again so that the laces of her corset were presented for him to loosen.

He kissed the space between her shoulder blades, above her chemise, the buss of his mouth on her bare skin making her nipples go tight. As quickly as his lips had branded her, they were gone, and then his fingers went to work on her corset. With efficient motions, he untied the knot and loosened her laces. She could take a deep breath again—the waspish waist she'd managed to affect for her evening gown had been lovely but not without its cost.

Her sides ached in relief as she caught the hooks in her hands and pulled them open. The corset dropped to the steadily growing pile of garments on the fine Axminster. Before she could prepare herself, he seized her waist again, spinning her to face him once more. Chemise, stockings, and drawers were all she had left, and his hungry gaze seemed to devour her, the naked desire on his chiseled countenance making her knees go weak.

"I'm not certain I can be tender," he said tightly, a muscle in his jaw ticking.

What a mystery he was, a man at odds with himself. Buttoned-up and starched and perfectly elegant. He hadn't removed a single garment of his own. It occurred to her then that she didn't want tenderness from him. She wanted a complete shattering of his control.

"Don't be, then," she said, reaching for his neck cloth, intending to untie it.

He caught her fingers, staying them. "I want you too much."

It was himself that he didn't trust, then, not her. And the knowledge was both a relief and a thrill.

"Let me," she said firmly, undeterred by all his warnings. "I want to help you disrobe."

"If I stay, I'm going to fuck you," he warned. "It won't be lovemaking."

Lucy had heard the vulgar term before. She'd read it in books. She knew the distinction he was making, and it didn't deter her.

She went to work on the knot of his neck cloth. "Call it whatever you like, husband. I want you here with me tonight."

He made a low, desperate sound, but his hands fell to his sides, his protest gone. She pulled the neck cloth away in one swift glide, and then she moved to his coat, sliding buttons free and pulling it away from his shoulders. The garment fell atop her discarded skirts. Her hands trembled slightly as she moved to his waistcoat, uncertain of herself and yet knowing she needed to show him her intent.

How strange it felt, touching him intimately—undressing him. Sliding cool buttons free of their moorings, running her hands over his shoulders, opening his shirt. He stood still and stoic for her ministrations, the intensity of his gaze searing her. More of his chest was becoming visible now, a breathtaking swath of masculine skin on display. He was solid and firm, his chest sprinkled with a fine smattering of hair. With great interest, her eyes followed the line of hair that disappeared below his waistband. And that was when she saw the thick, prominent ridge of him pressed against the fall of his trousers.

She hesitated, liquid heat an answering ache deep inside her.

"You're sure you want me here tonight?" he asked, a roughness in his voice that was so unlike the sleek, elegant aristocrat he ordinarily personified.

"Yes," she said.

He ripped the rest of his shirt away and shrugged it to the floor. Bare-chested and beautiful, he faced her. What a thrill to think this man was hers now.

"Touch me," he invited, the decadent rumble of his voice gliding over her like the finest silk.

Hesitantly, she placed her hands on his shoulders. He was hot and smooth and strong. Awareness burned through her, and she moved her touch lower, over his chest until he took one of her hands in his and dragged it down. He pressed her palm over the straining ridge in his trousers, and she felt him, long and impossibly large. Larger than she'd supposed he would be. The ache between her thighs intensified as she investigated him, tentatively at first and then with greater insistence, mesmerized by the way his body reacted to hers, growing harder, a rumble in his chest.

She liked this part of him, so different from her. Her curiosity and desire mingled, and she grew bolder, her fingers finding the closure on his trousers, sliding one button open. She wanted to see him, without the barrier of so much cloth. Wanted to feel him, bare skin on bare skin.

He took her wrist in a gentle grip, staying her.

"Not yet, or I'll lose control completely. I want you too much."

Gareth's words tempered her disappointment as he took her hand in his, guiding her to the bed. He kissed her, slowly, sweetly, and it didn't feel like *fucking* to her, what he was doing. It felt like a prolonged seduction. It felt like he wanted more from her than the mere act. Or maybe that was just what she longed for him to feel.

He kissed down her throat, stopping to grasp handfuls of

her chemise, then withdrew to lift it up and over her head. Cool night air kissed her breasts, her nipples puckering into tight buds that longed for his mouth on them. And as before in the garden, he lowered his head, taking the peak of one breast in his mouth and sucking.

A strangled moan left Lucy, because this was so much more delicious than what had happened before. In the lamplight, she could see him completely. His handsome face against her, his mouth on her, his tongue, his teeth... Oh heavens, his *teeth*. He nipped, planting one hand on her hip, while the other moved between them to find the buttons on the waistband of her drawers. The dainty silk glided down, landing on the floor, and he suckled her other breast while she stood before him in nothing more than stockings and garters.

She should have been embarrassed, but being naked with him felt natural. It felt right. And then suddenly, he moved again, dropping to his knees on the plush carpet, his hands on her hips coaxing her forward.

"What are you doing?" she asked, newly uncertain.

His beautiful face was so close to her sex, and there was nothing to shield her from his gaze.

"Kissing you," he said calmly, and then he made truth of his words.

Only, he wasn't kissing her on the mouth. He was kissing her *there*, and her knees started to buckle at the astonishing, glorious shock of it. Just a press of his mouth at first, but then something even more surprising—his tongue. The satiny, wet glide of it made her gasp, her hands flying to his broad shoulders for purchase to keep her from tumbling backward.

He made a dark sound of delight and probed deeper with his tongue, finding the bud hidden in her folds. He licked her, fast, dizzying strokes that sent unadulterated desire spiraling outward from the center of her body.

She'd read about this too, in the wickedest books she'd found. But no passage had sufficiently described what she was feeling now. She wanted to cry out, to grind herself into his face, to ask him for more. She wanted to lie down on the soft bed with him and bring him inside her. She never wanted him to stop this decadent torment.

He lifted his head, his icy gaze rising to meet hers, and the desire burning in those blue depths stole her breath.

His lips glistened in the low light. "Have I shocked you yet?"

She swallowed, trying to find the capacity for speech that had somehow been robbed from her. "No."

Was that what he was trying to do? Shock her into realizing she didn't want him? If so, he was going to be disappointed. Nothing he could do or say would persuade her otherwise.

Still holding her stare, he brought his mouth back to her sex, sucking so hard on her that this time, she did cry out and her knees buckled. He caught her, keeping her from falling, pinning her against the bed, and continued pleasuring her. She planted her hands on the bedclothes, surrendering herself to the glory of his wicked mouth between her legs.

She wanted to look away from him, and yet she couldn't break the hold his hot stare had on her. And part of her knew he wanted her to look her fill, to watch as he pleasured her, to watch his beautiful face nestled so close to her most intimate place, to know that he seemed to be reveling in it every bit as much as she was. Sensation washed over her, blinding and strong. He grazed her tender nub with his teeth and then ever so gently bit her there, and it was as if something inside her flew apart.

Mindless pleasure struck, leaving her breathless, clinging to the bed, halfway on it, halfway off. Wave after wave of it, his lips and tongue never leaving her until the last tremor of bliss finally subsided. And then he lifted her onto the bed as if she weighed scarcely anything, turning his attention to her garters and stockings.

He removed them quickly and efficiently, clearly a man who was familiar with a woman's undergarments. The thought sent a pang through her—jealousy, she supposed. She didn't want to think about Gareth with anyone else. Didn't want to know who had come before her, where he had learned his undeniable skill as a lover.

He kissed and caressed every bare expanse of skin he revealed, and then he shifted, tearing at the fall of his trousers. He didn't even bother to remove them, and she was treated to a momentary glimpse of his cock, large and erect, springing forth. And then he was guiding her legs apart, situating himself between them, and she felt the first glance of him over her swollen and tender flesh.

He moved above her, his dark hair falling over his brow, looking handsome and dangerous, some of his polish at last missing. His fingers dipped, parting her, seeking. She widened her legs, liking his touch on her, so deft and sure, different from his mouth and yet every bit as delicious. When he found her pearl and stroked, her hips jolted from the bed.

He took her breast in his mouth and sank a finger inside her. She gasped, the intrusion both strange and wonderful. He moved with ease, gliding through her wetness, and it felt so good to be filled in this way. The ache inside her renewed again, and she was restless beneath him, wanting, yearning, burning.

He dotted kisses over her breasts, along her clavicle, to her shoulder, that lone finger sliding in and out, deep and then retreating. The pressure was maddening. She wanted—needed—more. And she knew he would give it to her, but at his own pace. When he was ready. First, he would have her desperate and breathless, almost at the edge of coming completely apart.

He didn't speak. Didn't use comforting words, no reassurance, no tenderness. There was only action. The sound of their ragged breathing, his finger moving through her wetness. There was only sensation, the rasp of his stubble against her cheek as he nuzzled her temple.

She touched him everywhere she could, hungry for the feeling of his hard body, for his muscled strength. Shoulders and back, the tense musculature of his abdomen, over his bottom, firm and tight beneath the trousers he still wore. She tugged at them and pulled, wishing them gone, wanting him as naked as she was, but he was on his knees, and he withdrew from her, and suddenly there was the most delicious pressure at her entrance.

He thrust, and then he was inside her, so much bigger than his finger. She gasped at the rightness of it, the painful pleasure. There was a pinch, a sting as her body adjusted. He soothed her hip, kissed her neck.

"Relax, love," he murmured against her skin, his weight pinning her to the bed. "Let me in."

He was in, but apparently not fully. She discovered so in the next breath when he pushed farther, sinking deep inside her.

She gasped at the feeling of his cock buried within her. How right it felt, how strange and erotic, her hips cradling his, his chest pressed to her breasts. It was as if they were truly one, joined together in matrimony and now in body as well.

"You were a virgin," he said, lifting his head to stare down at her, a quizzical expression on his face.

Had he believed she wasn't?

"Yes," she agreed, body throbbing, pulsing, waiting for more.

The initial discomfort had subsided, and there was only desire now, burning hot and bright.

He kissed her cheek in a rare show of tenderness, his brow furrowed with concern. "Did I hurt you?"

"Only a bit," she said, threading her fingers through his hair, arching her back, the impulse to move overtaking her and making her restless.

There was more; she was sure of it.

And she wanted it.

"I'll have to make it better." His fingers went between them then, and his mouth returned to hers, urgent and demanding.

She tasted herself in his kiss. The play of his clever fingers over her bud made that spark of desire roar into a raging fire. He moved again, slowly, carefully, and the pressure inside her built. She was wet, so wet. He glided through that slickness with astonishing ease, and it was as if her entire body had been set alight. She kissed him, feeling as she did when she consumed too much wine. Lightheaded, drunk on him, on his mouth, his skin on hers, the weight of him atop her, his manly heat searing into her.

He strummed over her, his fingers taking her to that delicious edge of madness with ease. And she felt herself tightening on him in response. He thrust back inside, deep, so deep, and an acute sense of bliss threatened to shatter her. She moaned into his mouth, grasping at him as if she were drowning and he was the only lifeline keeping her afloat.

Because that was how it felt in that moment, her body coming undone, her mind fragmented. She was nothing more than sensation. Lucy closed her eyes and lost herself as he found a rhythm that made her desperate. He caught her legs and hitched them high around his lean hips and thrust into her again and again, with greater intent, never faltering, this time pinning her to the bed with the force of his weight, the possession of his cock.

She lost control, her inner muscles clamping down on him hard as another surge of bliss roared through her, brilliant gold lights flecking her eyes as she closed them tight and surrendered herself to desire. He stilled for a moment, his rigid length planted to the hilt, and it was the best feeling, unlike anything she could have imagined, a sensation that defied description. His chest pressed into her breasts, so deliciously close, their bodies entwined. Her heart hammered like a blacksmith on an anvil, this release even more potent than the last.

"Better?" he asked her, his voice strained, and then he rained kisses along her jaw, down her throat.

She realized he was breathless as well, that he was every bit as moved as she.

"Yes," she managed to say, somehow finding the ability to speak.

"Good." He gave one of her nipples a long, hard suck, and then he raised himself over her again, renewing his thrusts.

More? How could there be?

But there was.

She clung to him, moving with him, her body undulating, seeking. He seemed to finally lose the fragile grip on his control then, withdrawing from her only to slide fast and hard, filling her. And she understood what he'd meant with a sudden, blinding clarity—the difference between making love and fucking. There was nothing polite about what they were doing. It was ferocious and slightly desperate.

She loved every second of it.

He increased his pace, pushing into her, making her slide up the bed. And then he laced his hands together on her crown, leveraging himself on his forearms as he continued riding her, finding a place inside her she hadn't known existed, a place of such intensity that she couldn't keep herself from crying out, reaching yet another pinnacle.

She stopped slipping across the mattress when she reached the immovable rigidity of the headboard. His hands bore the brunt of his thrusts, keeping her head from slamming into the carved wood, his hips pumping faster and faster until he stiffened, and with a guttural sound, he emptied himself into her. She felt the hot rush of his seed bathing her, filling her, and her inner muscles spasmed again, more waves of pleasure unfurling.

Lucy held him to her, reveling in a new sense of intimacy, loving the way they were locked together, loving him inside her, atop her, his bare skin under her questing hands. But just as quickly as he had reached his pinnacle, he withdrew, rolling away from her, leaving her cold and naked in the bed.

Alone as he rose to his feet, moving across the chamber.

"Gareth?" she called after him, confusion chasing some of the languor that had stolen over her.

She wanted him to stay with her. Wanted him close. Wanted to curl around him, nestle against him. Never wanted him to leave.

"I'll leave you to your rest, madam," he said, his voice polite yet curt, his gaze averted.

And then, naked as the day he'd been born, he stalked from her room, closing the door adjoining their chambers with a terrible, final snap.

GARETH'S VALET was shaving him when there was a knock at the door. A hesitant knock, coming from Lucy's chamber. But he heard it just the same, because he was painfully aware of her presence, the separation between them nothing more than a slab of wood.

"My lord?" Trobridge asked, hesitating in his ministrations.

He had shaving soap on his face, lathered and ridiculous, and half his whiskers remained beneath, only one clean line of his jaw visible. He was also wearing only a dressing gown and drawers. A dangerous lack of garments if his wife was to be anywhere in proximity.

Wife.

What had once been a hated word, the cause of endless regret, now had a new meaning. It was strange to have someone inhabiting that role in his life again, someone in the chamber next door. The space was the same, and yet the room was vastly different. Much like the women. Anthea had been cold and aloof, hateful at times, bitter at others, and always shackled to her vices. Lucy was vibrant and warm, bold and brash and sensual in nature.

She terrified him, as did his inexplicable need for her. Gareth knew better than most the inevitable hell that a marriage could become. He needed to temper his need for his wife, to proceed with extreme caution. To keep her at a distance so that she couldn't inflict any damage upon him the way Anthea had.

"Gareth?" Lucy called from the other side of the door.

It popped open a crack in the next moment. He ought to have locked it. Next time, he would.

He cleared his throat. "I'm performing my morning routine," he told her.

"Lovely," she said, opening the door wider and breezing over the threshold, wearing a robe de chambre herself and looking eminently fuckable. "I'll just join you, then."

Had she thought he'd issued an invitation?

He frowned at her, Trobridge still hovering over him with

silent patience, stiff and formal. "Perhaps it can wait, Lady Rexingham. My valet is finishing my shave."

"I don't mind taking his place," she volunteered with a bright smile.

Gareth wasn't certain he liked the notion of Lucy anywhere near his throat with a razor. She hadn't wanted to marry him after all, and his new wife was decidedly unpredictable. To say nothing of the way he'd left her the night before after taking her virginity, which he'd been convinced she'd been relieved of some time ago.

His shock over her innocence and his body's reaction to her had led him to flee bare-arsed to his own room. He wasn't proud of the haste with which he'd decamped. Wouldn't blame her if she secretly harbored anger toward him for it, even if she did seem as if she hadn't a care in the world this morning.

Quite unlike the grim pall that had seized him in its grasp the moment he'd risen from a restless slumber.

"You needn't indulge me, my dear," he mildly rebuffed her, uncomfortably aware of her scrutiny and that of his valet as they awaited his answer. "Trobridge is happy to continue. I'll be with you presently."

"You don't think I would be good at it," she said shrewdly. "But you needn't worry. I'm a dab-hand at it. When my brother was injured in a horse race, I helped to shave him every day while he was an invalid."

He shouldn't be surprised she was a caring sibling; he'd seen the bond she shared with her sister Madeline. And yet, somehow he hadn't pictured her ever sitting by someone's sickbed, tending to them with loving concern. Anthea certainly wouldn't have done so. But then, she'd spent most of their marriage in the sickroom herself, wasting away.

Lucy had ventured across the room in her bare feet, lingering so close to his chair that her scent enveloped him.

"I appreciate your offer," he told her. "However, it isn't customary for a lady to trouble herself with her husband's morning schedule, aside from joining him for breakfast."

That seemed to give her pause as she angled her head at him, her emerald gaze searching his. "In England, Lord Rexingham, or in your particular household?" she asked. "If the former Lady Rexingham wasn't interested in attending you, it's no concern of mine. However, I should like to see you in the morning before greeting you at the breakfast table."

This was a discussion he didn't want to indulge before a servant, not even one as trusted and loyal as Trobridge.

Gareth turned to his valet. "Thank you. That will be all for now. I believe a private audience between Lady Rexingham and myself is in order."

The valet lowered his razor to the tray where shaving implements were neatly arranged. "Of course, my lord."

With a perfunctory bow, he was gone.

Leaving Gareth alone with his wife.

And half a face of shaving soap, he realized as he caught his own reflection in the bloody mirror. Surely she didn't truly intend to shave him. He wasn't certain he could bear for her to be that close. Not so soon after he'd lost all semblance of restraint last night and fucked his virginal wife across the bed like a feral beast.

Lucy moved behind him, her hands settling lightly on his shoulders, and he met her eyes in the mirror, willing his reaction to her touch to abate. "Isn't this ever so much nicer?"

Nicer? Her invasion of his private chamber and his morning ritual was anything but nice. It was damned irritating. He didn't need her particular brand of temptation at this early hour of the morning. If she lingered overly long, he feared he would cast all sense of propriety to the wind and spend the entirety of the day bedding her in as many ways as he could.

But he didn't dare reveal his weakness aloud. He'd learned in his previous marriage that vulnerabilities could be easily exploited.

"Perhaps you should inform me of what was so important that you chased my valet away before he could finish shaving me," Gareth told her coolly. "The soap is drying to my face."

"I wanted to wish you a good morning," she said cheerfully, bustling around the chair to the shaving implements, apparently undeterred. "I'll finish your shave. We can't have you going about with half a set of whiskers today, can we?"

"Trobridge would have finished it if he hadn't been interrupted," he said pointedly, trying not to take note of the way her breasts moved, free of the restraints of a corset beneath that dressing gown.

And failing.

Good Christ above, her nipples were hard under the thin fabric. Her entire trousseau was a collection of Parisian finery designed to turn every man within reach into a slavering, witless Satyr, he was sure of it. And it was working. Couldn't the woman have donned a sack this morning?

Something that buttoned all the way up to her nose?

"Are you always this devoid of cheer in the morning?" She wanted to know. "Perhaps you're hungry. I can ring for a tray of breakfast to be brought up for you. My father always goes into a rage when he's overdue for a meal, and when he's happily fed, he's docile as a kitten."

"Are you always this irritatingly jovial?" he countered.

In truth, his mood was typically thunderous when he failed to get enough sleep. And he'd certainly been lacking in slumber last night. Thanks to her this time, instead of the customary nightmares.

She took up the razor Trobridge had abandoned and

brought it alarmingly near to Gareth's face. "Hold still, dear. I'm going to finish this up, and I'd so hate to make you bleed."

"It isn't necessary," he protested.

"Oh, but it is. The soap is drying, just as you suggested. Besides, I have a lovely cream that I've perfected that goes on the face after a shave. I think you might enjoy it."

That *she'd* perfected?

"You mean to tell me you made it?" he asked.

"Of course." With a sunny smile, she stroked the razor along his jaw. "Who else would have made it? No, don't answer me. Hold still. This requires a delicate hand and a great deal of precision."

He adopted a grim silence as she continued shaving him, her motions soft and dexterous and not so very different from Trobridge's and yet unlike his in the most important way. His valet's morning shaves had never given Gareth a hard cock. But Lucy standing near, her breasts straining in his face as she leaned closer and brought the razor over his cheek, most certainly did.

He held his breath, trying not to breathe in her decadent scent. It was like a spell she had cast over him, giving her infinite power to wield. Anthea had never visited him in his chamber in the morning. He hadn't even supposed it was an action a wife might take. He still couldn't be sure if it was something ordinary and expected or if it was simply Lucy being, well...*Lucy*.

But inevitably, he had to breathe, and when he did, it brought her drugging scent deep into his lungs. She smelled like lily of the valley mingled with roses, and he wanted to bury his face in her throat and bury his cock inside her body at the same time, to devil with the day, with his shave, with everything and everyone.

He found himself admiring her. Her hair was plaited in intricate braids and swept away from her face—strange that although she hadn't bothered to dress, she had taken painstaking effort with her long, lush mahogany tresses. He wished they were unbound and hanging loose down her back so that he might sift the silken waves through his fingers. She was a beautiful woman, his new wife. And possessed of a lush mouth that haunted him even when she stood before him, catching her full lower lip in her teeth in her concentration as she finished running the razor along his jaw.

"Perhaps I should always carry a razor about with me," she suggested cheekily. "I find that I like having the ability to silence you."

"Hmm," he grumbled, all he could manage with the razor tracking below his jaw, approaching his throat.

She took her time, carefully finishing the work Trobridge had begun, and he did his best to remain still and to keep from reaching for her. Almost impossible feats, as it happened.

At long last, she must have deemed the torture she inflicted upon him enough, for Lucy removed the razor and surveyed her handiwork. "That will do, I think."

She rinsed the razor in a bowl of water Trobridge had laid out for the task, then took up a cloth and gently dried it, taking care with the pearl handle before folding it again. Then she moved to the shaving mug and soap with calm, efficient motions.

He cleared his throat. "Trobridge will tend to the shaving implements. You needn't toil like a servant."

"Yes, but if I didn't interrupt and toil like a servant, you'd likely have gone down to breakfast and disappeared on me," she pointed out, slanting a knowing glance in his direction.

In truth, he'd been planning to eschew breakfast and go to his club. To put some necessary distance between himself and the woman he wanted far too much. He rose from his chair, towering over her, and decided to wash his face to calm the heat suddenly burning under his skin.

"I'd hardly have disappeared," he denied curtly. "We live in the same household. You know where to find me if you have need of me."

"Perhaps I had need of you this morning," she said.

He threw water on his face, soaking his dressing gown, splashing it everywhere. God, did she want him to toss her into the bed behind him and have his way with her again? Hadn't she had enough?

But no, maybe she wasn't insinuating what he thought. Maybe she was saying she wished to converse with him, and it was merely his raging inner beast that persuaded him otherwise. Eyes closed, he felt about for the towel laid out by the wash basin. His fingers found hers instead, and the contact of her bare skin, so soft and smooth and warm, sent a jolt of unadulterated lust straight through him. What was she doing, following him about the room?

"Allow me," she said quietly, giving him his answer.

She had taken up the towel and was gently dabbing at his face, drying it. Gareth held still, unfamiliar with being tended to by a woman in such an intimate fashion. If she carried on, she was going to end up on her back with her dressing gown's hems around her waist.

He blinked, then took the towel from her, frowning. "I can finish myself, thank you, madam."

Gareth thought she might object or fight him over possession of the towel, but in the end, she relinquished it, though still remaining far too near for his comfort.

"Have I done something to displease you?" she asked.

And he felt like an utter cad.

He tossed the damp towel to the tabletop alongside the pitcher and bowl. "On the contrary. Everything about you pleases me far too well."

The admission was torn from him. He was loath to admit to her the effect she had on him. It felt as if he were ceding a great deal of power to her that he couldn't afford to lose. What was it about this vivacious American minx he'd married that had him forever at sixes and sevens?

"You have an odd way of showing it," she said, a tiny note of hurt in her voice that dismantled something inside him.

"Forgive me," he said, reaching for her then, his control shattered as it had been last night.

She came willingly, nestling in his arms, against his chest. Her arms went around him, her head tucked under his chin, and sweet God, it was the most natural position, and the rightness of her there made his chest seize.

"This is all new to me," he added, struggling to explain to her—hell, struggling to explain to himself.

"You were married before," she pointed out.

"Yes." He stiffened, uncertain of how to explain the hellacious muddle his marriage to Anthea had been. He hated that it affected him still, and yet he was powerless to extricate himself from the past's persistent grip. "The union was not a happy one," he managed tightly.

That was a vast understatement, for the union had been sheer misery. He'd grown to despise every second of each hour he'd spent bound to her as her husband.

Lucy said nothing for a few moments, her hands gently coasting up and down his back in slow, steady, reassuring motions. "Do you want to speak about it?" she asked at last, her voice hesitant.

He cleared his throat, disengaging from her. "No."

What he wanted to do was forget his nightmarish marriage with Anthea had ever existed. A difficult feat when it continually haunted him in his new role as husband to another.

Lucy's expressive face shuttered, and she moved away

from him. "Of course. Perhaps I should leave you to finish dressing, my lord."

He had pushed her away. Gareth hadn't meant to, but neither was he prepared to relive those terrible years. He couldn't do it. Not even for the sake of the lovely woman who was staring at him as if he were the source of her every disappointment.

"Yes," he agreed. "I will see you at breakfast, my dear."

The words were rusty. Panic was closing in on him. He had no intention of joining her at the breakfast room. She could dine with Bette. He had to get out of this house, out of his new wife's reach.

He could carry on with his day, carry on with his life.

The raging lust he felt for his wife didn't need to interfere.

"Until then," she said coolly, as if an invisible wall had been erected between them.

The moment she was gone, he took his cock in hand and stroked himself off to the thought of her beneath him, recalling how glorious she'd felt, tightening on him, coming undone for him. He came with a strangled groan he hoped she didn't hear, and then he hastily finished his morning routine, dressing as if he were attempting to flee a burning building and then taking his leave without passing the breakfast room.

CHAPTER 7

*L*ucy stared at her plate in silence, thinking it a pity that such an impressive assortment had been prepared by Rexingham's cook. She wasn't hungry, and her new husband had abandoned her.

She had postponed breakfast, believing he was delayed in his morning routine that she'd intentionally interrupted. But she'd had no choice but to concede defeat when she'd been informed that his lordship had left without word of when he might be expected to return.

Now, she was seated with Bette, who had no such qualms about consuming her hearty morning repast. Gareth's sister had already cleared half her plate.

"Are you not hungry?" Bette asked solicitously.

Lucy wondered if she ought to feign a smile for the other woman's benefit before deciding against it. This marriage had been Gareth's fault. His dratted insistence upon his sense of honor had propelled them into a union that neither one of them had wanted. And yet, while she had decided to carry on and give their marriage its best chance, he remained aloof and distant.

One would have thought she had been carrying some manner of contagious disease with the way he had been desperate to get away from her earlier in his room. Perhaps she shouldn't have intruded, but that was neither here nor there.

And his sister was staring at her expectantly, awaiting a response.

"I find I'm not particularly hungry at the moment," she said politely.

"I must say, it's very pleasant to have a companion here at the breakfast table," Bette said in conspiratorial fashion. "Anthea always took a tray in her chamber, although she scarcely ever consumed anything more than tea and toast with her morning laudanum."

Her morning laudanum?

Lucy frowned, considering her new sister-in-law with great curiosity. "Do you mean to say that the former countess took laudanum every morning?"

"And at lunch, dinner, and before bed," Bette elaborated. "Other times too, I should think."

Gareth's first wife had been an opium addict. Lucy was surprised. Of course, he had mentioned she preferred laudanum to the marriage bed. But Lucy hadn't understood the full implications of his revelation.

"Tell me," she said before she could think better of it, "did they ever have a happy marriage? Were they in love?"

She wasn't sure that it would matter, and she certainly didn't know the reason for her own interest. And yet, she couldn't help herself. Her husband intrigued her. She wanted to know more about him, about his past. Wanted to know everything there was, unlock all his mysteries and secrets. If such a feat were even possible, which she was very much beginning to doubt.

"I shouldn't speak out of turn," Bette hedged, biting her lip.

Guilt instantly assailed Lucy.

"I'm sorry," she hasted to say. "I shouldn't have placed you in such an awkward position. Forget that I asked, please."

"It isn't that I don't wish to tell you," Bette explained, "but that Gar is incredibly private about what happened with Anthea. It was a dark time in his life. I don't think he's ever recovered, not truly, even with her gone. It's also one of the reasons I'm so happy to see him marrying someone like you."

"Someone like me?" Lucy pressed a hand to her heart. "An American, you mean?"

Her sister-in-law smiled. "Not that, but I suppose where you come from may be part of what makes you so unique. You're bold and cheerful and kind, and I know that my brother is something of a proper bore, but there's far more to him than the face he presents to the world."

Lucy had no doubt there was, and she very much wanted to be able to see it. Wanted for her husband to feel comfortable enough to reveal his vulnerabilities to her. Earlier, when she'd had him at her mercy while she'd shaved him, she had reveled in her ability to crumble some of the walls he'd built around himself. Heaven knew she'd spent the night in her strange new bed tossing in twisted bedclothes, trying to think of ways she might keep him from putting distance between them.

Interrupting his morning routine had been a spur-of-the-moment decision, but it was a start. She intended to do it again tomorrow morning, and the morning after that, and the next day, too.

"Let's speak of something more convivial, shall we?" she suggested. "Your relationship with your brother is close, is it not?"

She had seen quite plainly at the country house party that

Gareth had doted on his sister, even fretting over the company she kept. The irony was still a source of reluctant amusement for Lucy. But she hadn't missed Bette's sobriquet for her brother either. It certainly suggested that Bette cared for her brother every bit as much as he loved her. And that closeness filled Lucy with not just warmth, but with hope too.

"Our parents died not long after Gareth and Anthea married," Bette said sadly. "So much responsibility fell on Gareth's shoulders. Suddenly, he was not just the earl, but he was my guardian, and he was also a new husband. He's been fretting over me ever since, but I love my brother dearly. He is a good man. He may seem frigid and reserved, but he's also what he's been forced to become. I hope you'll help him to break free of that mold."

Lucy wondered again what his marriage must have been like, what his life had been like before she had known him, to make him so detached. To make him balk at the slightest intimacy between them as husband and wife, aside from the purely carnal elements of sexual congress. He may be her husband, but he was also very much a stranger to her. Still, he wasn't always frigid. He'd proven so every time he took her in his arms. Each time his lips touched hers.

But she mustn't think of that now. Not when she was seated at the table with Gareth's sister, far too clever and observant for her own good.

"I can't make any promises," Lucy said gently, "but I'll try my best."

She meant those words. And she wanted her marriage with Gareth to become something more than a cold-blooded duty, the result of a shameless indiscretion in the moonlight when she'd thought him someone else. There was no mistaking him for anyone else now that she knew the pleasure of his lips on hers, his body taking hers.

"You're going to be good for my brother," Bette pronounced. "I just know you are."

Lucy hoped her sister-in-law was right, but if Gareth's actions this morning were any indication, she was going to have to fight him every step of the way.

CHAPTER 8

*G*areth sat in the chair before the crackling hearth in his study, gazing morosely into the flames. The glass of brandy he'd filled far too recently was already empty again. Which meant he needed another.

If he was going to keep his distance from his beautiful wife tonight as he very desperately needed to for his own self-preservation, then he'd probably need an entire goddamned bottle. Perhaps even two. At his present rate of pathetic besotted idiocy, nothing would keep him from stumbling to her chamber except getting so thoroughly inebriated that he wouldn't be able to ascend the staircase without falling down and breaking his neck. So foxed that he passed out in this wretchedly uncomfortable chair and woke at dawn with a neck that was as stiff as his randy prick.

He hadn't wanted to come home tonight.

No, he'd been doing everything in his power to avoid it. He'd gone to his club, visited old friends, had even received an invitation he would have accepted before that day in the Sherborne Manor gardens that had so thoroughly sealed his fate. Alice, Lady Harding, was a genteel, circumspect widow who had shared his bed often following Anthea's death. She'd invited him to spend the night with her in no uncertain terms.

But he was married to Lucy now, and if he'd been a faithful husband to Anthea, he'd be damned if he was anything less to the American firebrand he'd married. She was the only woman he wanted anyway, regardless of the fondness he'd once felt for Lady Harding. And that, too, was why he had stayed away.

Because he desired Lucy so much, it frightened him. His lack of control was alarming. He was a man who prided himself on tidiness, on pragmatism, on an orderly life in the wake of Anthea's death. His rigid grip on his own restraint had been the sole motivating force carrying him through the darkest days he'd faced. But it wasn't enough. Not when Lucy was within reach. Hell, not even when Lucy was above him somewhere, likely long since asleep in the haven of her bed.

Without him.

With a growl of frustration, he heaved himself from his chair, stalking across the room to the sideboard where a half-empty bottle of brandy beckoned. It wasn't the elixir that would save him, but it might prove enough to drown himself in, at least until the sun rose.

"Good evening, my lord."

Lucy's soft voice trilled down his spine like a caress.

Biting back an oath, he swiveled from the sideboard to find her approaching in an ethereal dressing gown and bare feet, her dark hair cascading around her in a mahogany cloud. Hercules rose from his cushion and bounded to greet her, jumping on his hind legs in his eagerness.

Gareth could relate.

Lucy favored the pug with a soft smile and gave his head an affectionate scratch. "Hullo there, my fine fellow. I missed you, too."

"Down, Hercules," he commanded sharply. "Be a gentleman."

The pug obeyed, casting a doleful glance in Gareth's direction before trotting back to his cushion and settling back down.

Gareth forced a bow in his wife's direction, trying to pretend as if he wasn't holding an empty glass in hand, as if he hadn't been sitting here in his study, avoiding her, finding himself at the bottom of a bottle of brandy.

"Lady Rexingham," he greeted in return, striving for formality between them, likely his only hope to keep from hauling her into his arms and carrying her to his bed like a rutting beast. "I thought you'd be long asleep by now."

A small smile curved her mouth. "Is that why you're lingering here in your study at such a late hour? I suppose you hoped I'd surrender myself to slumber and you could slip into your bedroom uninterrupted."

She was right, damn her, and it nettled that she could see through him so plainly. Anthea had never bothered to look.

"I didn't wish to press my attentions on you," he said coolly rather than acknowledging the accuracy of her assessment. "Last night was undoubtedly taxing for you. In such delicate situations, it's customary for a husband to be a gentleman and allow his wife her privacy."

He almost winced at the supercilious rot rolling from his tongue, a polite lie to cover up the fact that he wanted to fuck her more than he wanted his next breath. He wanted to fuck her here, on the carpet before the fire, with nothing but the heat of the flames and their own bodies to warm their skins. He wanted to fuck her against the wall, on this chair. He wanted her naked on top of him, underneath him. He wanted her on her knees. The depth of his need astonished him, made his hand shake as he splashed a measure of brandy into his waiting glass.

"I reckon I'll just have to join you here," she said, and then she was at his side, her diaphanous dressing gown brushing against his trousers, and he had to take a gulp of his brandy to keep from reaching for her.

Her scent surrounded him. And her hair... God, it was glorious. He flexed his fingers at his side, longing to run them through the thick, silken skeins.

Belatedly, he realized what she'd said. "Join me? You needn't, my dear. I do appreciate your wifely concern, but I'll adjourn presently."

She reached for the brandy, surprising him by pouring herself a glass. "I know I needn't, but I want to."

"That's brandy," he said, frowning.

Not a lady's drink, to be sure.

"I know." She shrugged. "I'm exceptionally talented at discerning one spirit from another."

She was mocking him. No one dared to do that. And he rather found it somehow amusing.

"A lady of many talents," he quipped, raising his glass to her in salute.

"Some of which you'd be surprised at," she added with a mysterious smile that made him want to kiss her.

His mind, already hindered by copious amounts of brandy, went to terrible places. But he knew that wasn't what she implied. He'd taken her virginity last night, for God's sake.

He tightened his grip on his glass. "Oh?" he managed to inquire politely, as if his cock wasn't suddenly raging in his trousers.

Stupid, filthy mind. His base nature seemed fated to forever get the best of him. Perhaps not entirely a misfortune, that. His first wife had been horrified by his sensual appetite; the second seemed blessedly open to it.

"I'm an excellent marksman," she said, apparently elaborating on her talents and not threatening to shoot him.

One never knew with an American.

"Do you hunt?" he asked.

He'd been to many shooting parties where ladies had ridden sidesaddle along with the gentlemen, their rifles at the ready.

"Never." She smiled brightly, lifting her glass back at him. "I haven't the heart for it. But having lived through the War of the Rebellion, my father decided it was important for all his daughters to know how to properly shoot a man."

How very bloodthirsty.

He blinked. "I shall consider myself duly warned."

Lucy took an elegant sip of her brandy, and he watched in fascination as her creamy throat dipped, and nary a cough nor sputter emerged. "I didn't say I would shoot you, my lord." She took another drink. "I've hardly had the provocation to do so…yet."

Gareth might have choked on his brandy if he hadn't already swallowed. "I'm heartily relieved, my dear."

Her smile deepened, and he felt the full effect of it like a blow to his midsection. "You know I'm joking, of course. You're far too handsome to shoot."

Now, he did cough, for he'd taken another draught and he hadn't expected such a tart rejoinder. She moved nearer, soundly clapping him on the back with a trifle more force than would have been strictly necessary.

"Are you well, my lord?" she inquired above his ragged, indrawn breath.

Only for him to dissolve into a coughing fit once more.

The strikes on his back lessened to soothing strokes. "Well enough," he wheezed. "Has anyone ever told you that you're a unique woman?"

He meant it as a compliment. She was so refreshingly

different from every woman he'd ever known. And as for Anthea—sweet God, Lucy was like the sun, whereas his former wife had been the moon.

"I pride myself on it," Lucy said, then sobered, her gaze turning searching. "We missed you today, my lord."

He supposed that by *we*, she meant herself and Bette.

"I trust you and my sister are getting along well," he said, studiously avoiding the underlying question in her voice.

She wanted to know where he'd been and why. Wanted to know the reason for his disappearance. He didn't blame her. She was his wife, and he certainly owed her an explanation. The trouble was, he hadn't arrived at one himself just yet, and he didn't know what the devil to tell her.

"We are getting along in a lovely fashion." Lucy took another sip of her brandy, eyeing him somberly. "Despite my *unsuitable influence*."

Her pointed words had their intended effect, sinking into him like a barb. "Lucy, I'm sorry. I never should have said that."

"Do you regret marrying me?" she asked, her emerald eyes still searing him with their intensity.

Probing. Seeing far too much.

Did she imagine that was the reason for his absence today? If so, he hated it. Hated himself for having caused her a moment of pain.

"I regret the hasty actions that necessitated our nuptials," he said carefully. "But I hardly regret taking you as my wife. It was the honorable thing to do after I so thoroughly dishonored you."

Her lips tightened, and she moved away from him, returning to the sideboard to pour another splash of brandy into her empty glass. "How heartening."

He had intended for his words to be honest, if not particularly romantic. But then, he wasn't a romantic man. And surely Lucy had no disillusions about the reason for their hasty union. Still, he felt a pang of unease deep inside him, cutting through the brandy-induced fog soaking his brain.

He went to her, joining her not for the brandy but because he wanted to be nearer. "I suppose I might ask the same of you. Do you regret marrying me, Lucy?"

"You know I didn't want to be married," she reminded him softly. "I wouldn't say it's cause for regret. What's done is done, and we can't change it. But I never envisioned myself being a lord's wife."

"What *did* you envision for yourself?" he asked, curious and strangely defeated by her response.

Which was foolish, because what had he expected? A declaration of undying love and devotion? He had been the one to force her hand, to insist upon marriage. She'd been vehemently opposed to the notion.

"I wanted to travel," she said wistfully. "To see the world. To start a business of my own. Beyond that, I'm not sure. My mother was so determined to see Madeline and me married to aristocracy, and now it seems I've granted her that wish."

He took another sip of his brandy, studying her, thinking her far too lovely for his peace of mind. "You don't want to be a countess, then?"

"I'm far too accustomed to being Lucy Chartrand, I suppose." Another small smile curved her lips, didn't reach her eyes. "I'll grow used to being the Countess of Rexingham with time, I'm sure. And perhaps also with the presence of my husband to facilitate the new position."

So, they were back to his disappearance. He had known he would have to answer for it eventually. Perhaps he ought to try now.

"I had some matters to attend to," he tried, aware of how stiff and formal he sounded.

"Do you have a mistress?" she asked frankly. "Is that

where you were this evening? You can answer me plainly. I'm not unfamiliar with such matters. It's just that I had hoped you might not resort to that sort of arrangement. At least, not given the newness of our union."

"I don't have a mistress," he answered honestly. "If I demand your fidelity, then I must also offer my own in return."

Some of the stiffness left her bearing. "What kept you from us all day, then? Or is that question *de trop* for a bride to ask her husband?"

He raked his free hand through his hair, wondering how to respond. "I'm afraid I don't know how to be a good husband to you, Lucy. My previous marriage was..." His words trailed off as he searched for the appropriate descriptor. Hateful came to mind. So, too, wretched. In the end, he settled for something less vehement. "My previous marriage was unhappy. I'm loath to begin our union in the same vein, and yet I'm terrified that I'm doomed to repeat the past."

Gareth had revealed far more than he'd wanted. Far more than he'd even been aware he was feeling. But then, no doubt it was the brandy, loosening his tongue, making him aware of emotions kept firmly trapped beneath the surface, tamped down and locked away no longer.

For a moment, Lucy said nothing. Simply stared at him. And then she startled him yet again by taking his hand in hers and lacing their fingers together.

"Come," she said. "Let us sit by the fire. This conversation feels far too heavy to have standing up."

He didn't disagree. And yet, how strange it felt, to have a wife who wanted to speak to him. To touch him. A wife who looked at him with kindness in her eyes instead of disdain.

She gave his fingers a reassuring squeeze as he allowed himself to be meekly led to the chairs positioned by the fire.

Lucy guided him to the chair he had so recently abandoned. "Sit, if you please."

"It's bad form to sit in the presence of a lady," he pointed out.

"No one is here to watch and judge us," she countered.

Gareth sat.

Lucy settled in the seat to his right, their hands still entwined. "There. That wasn't so dreadful, was it?"

He stared into the dying embers of the fire, which seemed a far safer place to direct his attention than on his stunning wife. "Not particularly, no."

"Why did you marry her?" she asked quietly.

His gut clenched at the reminder of the past. But he owed Lucy something. More than he'd given her thus far, and he knew it.

"Obligation," he offered, forcing himself to remember, to return to the days when he'd been young and idealistic enough to make colossal mistakes. "Duty. Our families had made it clear that they expected a match between us. I wanted very much to gain my father's approval, which I later learned was unattainable, and most definitely wasn't won by throwing myself into a doomed marriage with a woman who tolerated my presence on the best of days and despised me on the worst."

"I'm sorry," Lucy said quietly, stroking his hand with the soft pad of her thumb. "I know what it's like to want to win the favor of your parents. My father's first love is his business, and the rest of us receive the crumbs of his affections like geese being fed at a pond. A few bits here and there that we must scrabble over."

He heard the sadness in her tone and wondered what kind of man her father was. They had met briefly on the occasion of their wedding, but Mr. William Chartrand had almost immediately departed on a steamer bound for New

York after attending the ceremony. He'd been tall and brash, and Gareth had instantly seen where Lucy's dark hair and green eyes had come from. Aside from those two traits, he hadn't been able to find many similarities.

"And your mother?" he asked. "What is your relationship with Mrs. Chartrand like?"

Whilst he'd seen far more of Lucy's interactions with her mother, he didn't know much about her, aside from her reputation in society as a woman determined to secure her daughters noble husbands.

"She is every bit as removed," Lucy answered, "but in a different sense. If my father's true love is his business, then my mother's is all the money and power it's attained. She adores society. The way she's seen is of the utmost importance. It's why she wanted Madeline and me to marry aristocrats. But that's quite enough about me. I want to know more about you, my lord."

"Gareth," he reminded her, and he wasn't sure why. Her calling him by his Christian name would only engender a greater sense of intimacy between them. He should want to avoid it at all costs.

"Gareth," she repeated in her husky voice.

And his cock twitched. Heaven help him.

"What made your marriage an unhappy one?" she ventured.

Thinking about Anthea again had a dousing effect on his desire.

He took a bracing sip of his brandy, mulling the answer. "The more apt question might be what didn't make it an unhappy one. Both of us were to blame. I married Anthea scarcely knowing her. We were mutual acquaintances suddenly thrown together and forced to share a life. She was already addicted to opium when we married, which didn't help matters. It soon became apparent that I'd married an invalid who was content to hide herself away in her chamber, growing increasingly dependent on the solace she found in laudanum."

He paused, the old misery unraveling inside him, the helplessness he'd felt, the battle he'd fought to help Anthea, one he'd inevitably lost. It was almost a shock to realize that the secrets he'd kept hadn't died with her. He'd simply buried them deep, hoping they'd never resurface.

"Oh, Gareth," Lucy said, her voice laden with sadness. "I had begun to wonder, after what you told me last night and then Bette's hints this morning at breakfast. Little wonder your past marriage made you miserable."

He turned to find her watching him, not with pity as he had feared, but with understanding and concern.

"I wanted to help her," he elaborated. "I brought doctors to her. I did everything I could as best as I knew how. But she couldn't be helped. In the end, the opium claimed her just as I feared it would. We were living separate lives by that point, and I'd resigned myself to the fact that I would never have children. I'm ashamed to admit it, but in some ways, her death was a relief."

"You were finally free," Lucy said.

And he couldn't deny it. His marriage had been a burden for so long, one he had stoically carried with him each day. One he had protected and hidden. He'd taken great pains to make certain Anthea hadn't been the subject of gossip. Any servant who had dared to carry a hint of a tale had been summarily sacked. He'd ruthlessly quashed every whisper.

"I don't know if I'll ever be free of it," he admitted, and that concerned him every bit as much as his reaction to his new wife did. "I thought I would be able to put it aside, but the truth is, I don't know how to be the husband you deserve. I shouldn't have married you. Heaven knows I never should have kissed you in the gardens that day. Nor afterward."

"Perhaps we can find our way together," Lucy suggested.

His brave, daring wife who had so wanted to avoid the society marriage her matchmaking mother desired that she'd been willing to cause a scandal with a footman. Instead, she'd found herself neatly trapped in just the sort of arrangement she'd been seeking to avoid. He wanted to believe they could find the way together. That there could be a future for them, one that wasn't bleak and hopeless. But he'd also experienced the inevitable disappointment life wrought.

He took her hand and brought it to his lips, kissing her knuckles. "I fear you'll need patience for me, Lucy."

"I can be a very patient woman," she said, "when it's asked of me."

He thought he might beg in that moment. But instead, he pressed his lips reverently to her palm. "I'm a fortunate man."

CHAPTER 9

*L*ucy waited in the shadows of the carriage Gareth had ordered to await him following breakfast and did her utmost to bolster her rapidly flagging courage.

She couldn't help but to feel she was fighting a losing battle.

Three days into her marriage, and the scorching lover of her wedding night had been replaced by a cool, distant, polite gentleman yet again. One who deferred to her sweetly in all matters, always declining to join her beyond a morning repast, before disappearing for the day.

You may consult with Cook, my dear, he told her the morning after their moving conversation in the study. *I'll eat whatever you choose for the menu.* And then he'd taken his hat and coat and gone out the front door before she could protest.

You may attend the Lady's Suffrage Society meeting without me, darling, he told her smoothly the next afternoon, already dressed in evening finery. *I have other plans for the night.* What those plans had been, she'd never know. Her husband had neither divulged them nor offered to invite her to partake in them.

I won't be home for dinner tonight, he informed her at breakfast the third day. *You and Bette needn't keep the meal waiting for me.*

And so it went. A litany of excuses for keeping her at a safe distance, the door adjoining their bedrooms kept carefully locked from his side. She couldn't intrude on his morning ablutions without the key, and he knew it. She couldn't speak with him when he was nowhere to be found. Couldn't kiss him when he was forever flitting from one place to the next in the manner of a shadow.

She *wanted* to kiss him.

She wanted to more than kiss him.

But she couldn't very well do either of those things if he continued to hide from her. And that was why she had decided to turn the tables on him just a bit. It was her turn to hide. Only, she was running toward him instead of away from him.

The muffled sound of her husband's voice reached her at last, followed by the thump of his feet on the carriage steps. She braced herself for his displeasure. The door opened, cool air and early morning gloom streaming in.

Her husband was halfway into the carriage when he froze, his gaze meeting hers.

"I beg your pardon, my dear," he said as if he were a stranger in a ballroom instead of the man who had shared her bed. "I didn't realize you had requested a carriage as well. I'll just have the brougham brought round."

"That won't be necessary," she said briskly.

He frowned. "Of course it will. I don't mind taking the smaller conveyance. The landau is much more comfortable for a lady in skirts."

"It is also much more comfortable for a husband and wife to travel in together," she said, forcing a smile.

"I'm sure our destinations aren't similar, dear."

"And I'm sure they are," she countered. "I'm going where you're going."

"Lucy," he began to protest.

But she wasn't having any of it. "Get in," she commanded, the same tone she used for Hercules.

And like his cunning pug, Gareth responded to it, grimly finishing ascending the carriage steps and tucking his tall frame onto the Morocco leather squabs opposite her. Pinning her with an icy stare, he rapped on the carriage roof. The vehicle lumbered into motion.

"I would imagine you're not the first woman to enter the Black Souls," he said. "But you may well be the first lady."

Lucy knew what he was speaking of, naturally—the Black Souls club was a rather notorious establishment owned by Mr. Elijah Decker. He and his wife, Lady Josephine, had also been in attendance at Sherborne Manor. Lady Jo, as she was more familiarly known, was a leading member of the Lady's Suffrage Society as well.

"Surely Mr. Decker's wife has been there," she suggested, attempting to sound unperturbed.

Was that where he had been these last three days, hiding away at a club all morning, afternoon, and evening?

"I wouldn't know if she has," Gareth told her, resting his hand on his knee and idly drumming his long, elegant fingers one by one in a steady rhythm.

As if he were bored.

Or bothered by her presence.

She hoped it was the latter rather than the former, but she was prepared for either.

"I suppose I should be thankful you haven't been spending your days with women other than your wife at the club," she said brightly before fanning herself. "Oh my. It is exceedingly warm in here, isn't it?"

"Mmm," was all her husband said, a noncommittal hum.

But his eyes were on her, steady and intense. She seized her inner sense of boldness, sensing that if she wanted to win her husband over, she couldn't sit idly by as he continued to hide from her and dwell in the pain of his last marriage instead of looking to their future. No, indeed. She was going to have to help him break the ties of the past, one by one.

"Quite warm," she lied blithely, removing her wrap and then undoing a handful of buttons on her demure bodice. "I do so wish I had a fan. Perhaps I can procure one at your club."

He cleared his throat, his gaze dipping to follow the swells of her breasts, just barely visible where her bodice began to gape. "I don't think you'll find any fans or other ladies' fripperies at the Black Souls."

"What will I find there?" Slowly, steadily, she moved to the ties on her hat, undoing the ribbons before setting it aside. "This is a bit better. It's hotter than a New York summer in here, and I don't mind telling you, New York summers are warm enough to roast the devil himself."

As she said the last, she moved to her gloves, tugging at the silk of first one, then the other, and removing them.

"I'm not at liberty to divulge what you'll find there," Gareth said, his voice low and husky. "The members are sworn to secrecy, and the club is a private one."

"And you've spent nearly all the waking hours of each of the last several days there," she said, unable to keep the bite from her tone as she recalled his many and extended absences.

"Not all the waking hours," he murmured.

And that rather stung.

But she reminded herself that, by his own admission, he

didn't have a mistress. Even if he wasn't at his club, he hadn't been with another woman. At the moment, she would take what she could get where he was concerned. And that meant she had this carriage ride.

Both her gloves were off. He'd turned his attention to the window and the city passing by beyond it. That wouldn't do.

"The sun is shining on me," she announced. "That is what is making me so terribly overheated. I'll just move to your side of the landau."

Without waiting for his response, she shifted herself—not an inconsequential feat given the cramped confines of the carriage and the abundance of her bustle. And yet, she managed it, wedging herself beside him, her skirts crushing into his impeccable trousers.

"It's raining, Lucy," he pointed out calmly.

His attention had returned to her, his gaze seeming suddenly hungry and dark.

"And?" she asked, sliding another button on her bodice free.

He swallowed hard, and she watched in great fascination the way his Adam's apple bobbed. "You couldn't have been sitting in the sunshine. The sun isn't shining."

"It *was* shining," she countered, determined. "I'm sure of it. Perhaps it's gone behind a cloud for now."

"The same clouds that have been blotting out the sky since the sun attempted to rise this morning?" he asked, a sharp note in his voice.

He certainly wasn't making her plot easy, was he? Apparently, Gareth had rediscovered his restraint wherever he'd misplaced it on their wedding night. But she intended for him to lose it again.

One of her dearest friends in New York City, Miss Idalia Parish, had a mother who was something of a crusader. All her servants were reformed criminals, much to the horror of

122

high society. Her butler was a former pickpocket, and he'd regaled Idalia, Lucy, and Madeline with various sleights of hand. Lucy hadn't forgotten those skills, and occasionally, they still proved quite useful.

"Have the clouds been out all morning?" she frowned at her husband, feigning confusion. "Oh dear, I hadn't noticed. It's not raining now, however."

He turned instinctively to gaze out the window to ascertain the veracity of her claim, and Lucy hastily reached a hand behind her to undo the clasp of her necklace. The heavy Chartrand diamonds fell down her corset and between her breasts.

"It's decidedly still raining, my dear," he said, swinging his stare back to her, only to stiffen at her side. "What are you doing?"

"My necklace has come undone," she said with pretend distress, tucking her hand down her bodice. "I do believe it's fallen into my corset, but my fingers aren't long enough to retrieve it."

That was a lie, and she was sure they both knew it. But she wasn't above using subterfuge to get what she wanted. In this case, him.

She'd be damned if she allowed him to hide away in his club all day and night without her.

"Damn it, Lucy," he growled, a new warning entering his voice.

One that told her he wasn't just irritated with her. She had broken through his cool shell. Shattered his control.

The lover of the midnight gardens and their wedding night had returned.

She held his gaze, tension crackling between them like lightning. "Will you help me?"

His jaw tensed, his hot stare falling to her opened bodice. "Try to fetch it yourself."

She might have known he would prove stubborn, despite his obvious reaction to her. Lucy slipped her fingers inside her chemise, into her corset, not even attempting to reach the necklace that was lodged heavy and cool between her breasts before withdrawing.

"I can't," she told him with what she hoped was believable contrition.

His gaze darkened. "I'm sure your corset is laced too tightly for my hand to fit down it. My hands are quite large."

Oh, she knew that. Large and strong and capable. She loved those hands on her body.

"Fine," she said, reaching for the buttons on her bodice.

"What are you doing?" he asked, his voice husky and deep.

She undid a few more buttons. "If you won't aid me, then I'm going to have to disrobe so that I can retrieve the necklace myself."

"Disrobe in the carriage?"

He sounded incredulous. She would have smiled had the moment been any less serious.

"How else am I to rescue my necklace?"

"Jesus," he gritted. "Stop that, Lucy."

"Stop what?" she asked innocently, her fingers still flying over the tidy row bisecting her bodice.

"Opening your damned bodice." This time, his voice was a growl as he moved at last, catching her hands in his and staying them. "I'll do it."

"You'll open my bodice?"

It was almost entertaining, watching his struggle. Lucy knew she was winning in this battle they waged. But he was being terribly stubborn and refusing to admit defeat.

"No," he growled. "I'll fetch the necklace."

And then he unceremoniously stuffed his hand down the front of her corset.

～

Ah, God.

Skin.

Warm, soft, silken skin.

Gareth's restraint shattered the moment his hand dipped inside Lucy's bodice and he touched her. She'd been toying with him. Playing some manner of game only she understood the rules to, and he'd known it. Driving him to the edge of reason with her undone buttons and her necklace down her damned corset.

But none of that mattered now.

Not even the gold and diamonds his fingers easily brushed over and pulled free of their temporary home between her luscious breasts. The necklace was of little concern to him. All he wanted was her.

He tossed the heavy, priceless piece of jewelry to the squabs opposite them as if it were worthless. And then he hauled his tempting wife into his lap. She made a noise of startlement as her hands settled on his shoulders, keeping herself from flying to the carriage floor as they jostled over a bump. Her eyes were wide and sparkling, twin pools of emerald that he wanted to lose himself inside.

"What are you doing?" she asked breathlessly.

"What you wanted me to do," he said, and then he cupped her nape and drew her head down to his.

Her lips parted, and he deepened the kiss instantly, giving her his tongue. She sucked on it, making a sweet sound of surrender, and his cock went rock hard in his trousers. She was a tempting weight on his lap, the burden of far too many layers of garments keeping him from what he wanted most. For a wild moment, he thought about her riding his cock here in the carriage. Of taking her fast and rough while his coachman unwittingly drove them to their destination.

But no, he didn't fuck in carriages.

Or did he?

He slipped his hand inside her opened bodice, cupping the swell of her breast so deliciously spilling over the edge of her corset. Gareth had been trying his best to resist her. To resist the flames of desire that threatened to become a conflagration. And now she'd stowed away in his damned carriage and had begun undressing herself.

He was helpless to do anything other than succumb.

Maybe he could fuck her, here and now. It would be quick. He could get this poison out of his blood and carry on with his day.

She was a vixen, a Siren. He never wanted to stop kissing her. How had he ever thought he could marry her and then keep a polite distance? There was no distance he could manage to maintain. He wanted all of her, every seductive, bold, brazen part. He wanted to consume her, to possess her, to make her his in a thousand different ways.

He dropped his hand to her skirts, clenching a handful of silk, and dragged her hems higher. The confines of the carriage didn't allow for much room, but there was enough. His palm coasted over her stocking-clad calf and then higher, finding the split in her drawers. She was seated atop him as if she were riding sidesaddle, which gave him convenient access to everything he desired. He parted the slit.

A moan tore from him. He couldn't help it. She was hot, sleek, and so deliciously wet. He swirled her dew over her, finding her swollen clitoris. Her legs parted wider, enough so that he could trace her seam all the way to her entrance and slide his finger inside her drenched cunny. She felt so good, tightening on him, drawing him deeper, and he wanted far more. He wanted his cock gliding through that wetness.

Desire pumped through him, an all-encompassing need.

But then he remembered how new she was to lovemaking. He couldn't shag her in a carriage. She wasn't an experienced lover. He had to remind himself to go slowly, to be tender with her. He broke the kiss, allowing his head to fall back as he exhaled on a ragged breath. But he couldn't stop touching her. His thumb found her pearl, circling, teasing. His finger dipped in then out in a steady mimicry of what he wanted to do with his cock.

How beautiful she looked, thoroughly debauched, her lips swollen from his kisses, her bodice undone, breasts pressed high by her corset, her skirts rucked up, his hand beneath them. If he'd been a painter, he would have wanted to capture this moment, the desire in her eyes, the way her body was his for the taking.

He wanted to make her come. Wanted her writhing and helpless with pleasure.

He set himself to the task, wishing she were naked. Wishing they were in a bed instead of this blasted carriage, that he could thoroughly gorge himself on her until they were both sated and passed out in sensual oblivion. But that wasn't to be, because he'd stupidly left for the Black Souls this morning just as he had the previous mornings. Because he was running from her and everything she represented.

And what had Lucy done? She'd run after him.

Time for her reward.

She leaned forward, pressing a kiss to his jaw, then his throat, rubbing her cheek against his like a cat. He added a second finger, pumping them in and out, curling them, finding a place he knew would drive her wild as he continued to strum over her pearl.

"Is this what you wanted?" he asked her, her breath falling in hot pants against his neck. "Tell me, Lucy. Is this the reason you undid all those buttons and pretended your necklace came undone on its own?"

He was aware of her ruse. She'd directed his attention to

the window, and then with the expert ease of a common thief, she'd unclasped the jewels and sent them dropping into her corset. He'd been determined not to lose his control, but she'd pushed him too far. And now he was going to give her what she'd asked for.

"I...oh," she said on a moan as his fingers glided deep again, the wet sounds of him pleasuring her mingling with her ragged breaths in the quiet of the carriage.

"Did you sneak into my carriage so that I would have no choice but to make you come?" he asked, turning his face toward her, catching her earlobe in his teeth and biting.

"What if I did?" the minx asked, entirely unashamed.

And damn him if it wasn't the most potent aphrodisiac, her unabashed acceptance of her own sensuality, her desires. She wanted him. His firebrand, who had charmed her way through men on two continents and across a vast ocean in between, wanted him. It seemed nothing short of a miracle.

If he wasn't inside her in the next five minutes, he would perish of the endless, aching, all-consuming need.

He continued stroking her, kissing her throat, breathing in her sweet scent, reveling in the husky sounds she was making as he pleasured her. "Are you tender here, Lucy? I don't want to hurt you, but I need to be inside you. Badly."

So badly that if this continued, he was going to spend inside his trousers like a callow youth. But he didn't dare say that aloud. He'd already swallowed enough of his pride when he'd hauled her into his lap and demonstrated just how appallingly weak his restraint was.

"Yes," she whispered, rocking against his hand. "Please, Gareth. I want you, too."

Sweet words. Forbidden words. Words that wrapped around him like an embrace. Words he tucked deep inside himself for later, when his mind wasn't so addled by lust and he could make sense of this confusing desire burning within him.

He guided her legs, helping her shift so that she was astride him.

"This way?" she asked, sounding shocked and dubious, but also intrigued.

And a fresh wave of lust washed over him at the innocence in that question. She may glory in her own sensual nature, but she was still new to lovemaking. He couldn't wait to show her. To teach her.

"This way," he repeated, caressing her hips. "Stay on your knees and hold your skirts."

It was no easy feat. The carriage swayed over a rut in the road and nearly sent her toppling to the floor, but he held her there, keeping her from harm with one hand as he undid the fall of his trousers with the other. His cock sprang free, erect and demanding, and he stroked himself, his ballocks already tightening with the need for release.

"Now bring yourself down on me," he instructed, guiding her again, pulling her lower, until the head of his cock brushed over her drenched folds, and he couldn't bite back a moan of pure, animalistic bliss. He teased her swollen pearl, then slicked his erection up and down her slit before pressing against her opening, scarcely refraining from ramming hard and deep. "Sit on me, Lucy. Take me inside you."

She obeyed, hesitantly descending to his waiting cock, and suddenly the tip of him was burrowed in decadent heat and soft, wet feminine flesh. And it was good, so bloody good. It was also so wrong, fucking her in his carriage like this, as if she were a common doxy instead of his wife. The coachman might hear it. They might arrive at the club at any moment. But somehow, those realizations only made him harder.

Lucy let out a breathy moan that was laden with wonder, sinking down on him more fully. He was surrounded by her tight, slick cunny, but there was more. He wasn't quite all the way inside her.

"More," he rasped. "Take more of me."

And somehow, she did. She lowered the rest of the way, impaling herself on his cock, and he was engulfed in pure sensation. Hot, velvet wetness.

"Like this?" she asked breathlessly, her ripe breasts suspended before his face like an offering he couldn't resist.

He removed his hand from under her skirts and used it to tug at her bodice, at her corset, pulling it down until one creamy breast emerged, the pink nipple at its peak hard and waiting for his mouth. Gareth bent his head, sucking before withdrawing.

"Just like that, sweetheart," he managed to say. "Only, you'll need to move."

"Yes," she agreed raggedly. "Show me how."

"Ride me." Clamping his hands back on her waist, he instructed her how to move, helping her to find a rhythm that drove them both wild. She rose to her knees, his cock almost sliding from her body, only to slam down on him hard.

"Oh, Gareth," she moaned, tightening on him, her body more than ready.

"This is what you wanted when you waited for me in this carriage, didn't you?" he asked, his hips pumping against hers, chasing her, needing more, needing everything.

Her surrender. Her climax. To come inside her.

She didn't answer him, only moaned.

But he wanted her confession. He wanted her to admit that she hungered for him, that he wasn't alone in this mad, furious desire.

"Say it," he demanded, thrusting up into her, losing control. "Tell me, Lucy. You wanted my cock inside you."

"Yes," she gasped out, her cunny clamping on him hard as her orgasm barreled through her. "I wanted you."

He held her as she shattered, her sheath convulsing on him, milking his cock as she collapsed against his chest. And then he pumped into her again, filling her, sinking deep. As the carriage rocked to a halt, he spilled inside her with a harsh cry, coming so hard that tiny black stars speckled his vision, the huge diamonds on her necklace twinkling at him mockingly from the opposite squabs.

CHAPTER 10

"You want bacon, don't you?" Lucy asked.

Hercules sat at her side, gazing up at her in an adoring fashion she was beginning to wish his master would imitate. At her question, he let out a happy bark.

She held a bite of bacon aloft. "Bacon?"

Bark, bark.

"Stay sitting like a gentleman," she warned gently. "Or you can't have any."

Hercules blinked at her, gazing at her with chocolate eyes.

Lucy slowly lowered the bacon toward his nose, gratified when the pup remained on his rump as she'd requested. "Now."

He opened his mouth and caught the bacon, making a loud, smacking sound that delighted her.

She patted him on the head. "What a good boy you are."

Bette chuckled from across the breakfast table. "You've worked your magic upon him. I vow, before you came to Claremont House, that little beggar was terrorizing the household, and now he's as polite as any prince."

If only she had been able to work her magic upon Gareth in the same fashion, Lucy thought wryly.

"I'm not sure I worked any magic on him," she denied. "He merely needed the proper incentive to listen."

"Bacon is a decidedly excellent one," Bette agreed, smiling. "You ought to dangle some in my brother's direction and see if you can bring him to heel." The moment the words emerged from her sister-in-law, Bette clapped a hand over her mouth, her eyes going wide. "Oh, do forgive me, Lucy dear. I spoke without thinking."

Lucy returned her attention to the remnants of breakfast on her plate, smiling sadly at her poached egg and bacon. "You needn't apologize, Bette. You haven't said anything I haven't thought to myself. Believe me, I do so wish your brother might be led about with nothing more than a piece of bacon."

As it was, the only lure he'd responded to was herself.

But she wasn't about to confide that in Gareth's sister.

And while she was pleased to find one vulnerability lurking beneath her husband's frigid exterior, and although she enjoyed their lovemaking far more than she would have imagined possible, she'd also come to realize, a month into their marriage, that it wasn't sufficient.

She didn't want to be ignored unless she seduced her husband.

She didn't want to spend her days with no one but Hercules and Bette for companionship, instructing the servants and existing in the gilded cage that was Claremont House. She adored Gareth's pug and his sister both. But she missed her sister, her friends. She missed working on her creams.

She missed the dreams she'd once had for herself.

She felt hopelessly adrift in this new life. By night, her husband brought her body to life and pleasured her in ways she'd never known existed. But by day, he retreated again, disappearing to wherever he wished, whether it was to his club or his study or the homes of his friends. She had hoped for something more in their time together. Had foolishly believed that, given the passage of time, Gareth might be more inclined to release his grip on the past and let her into his mind, his life, perhaps even his heart.

Certainly, something more than just his bed.

"Is he being kind to you?" Bette asked softly, interrupting Lucy's troubled musings.

"Of course," she was quick to answer. "Your brother is a most polite and solicitous man when he chooses to be."

Some of the harshness had faded since their wedding, and she was grateful for that. But there still remained so many walls she needed to break down. So much ice that required melting.

"But polite and solicitous isn't exactly enough to make a wonderfully happy marriage, is it?" Bette asked shrewdly.

Lucy sighed. "Perhaps in time, it can be."

"Oh, Lucy," her sister-in-law said, frowning. "You are the sister I've always wanted, and I've hoped for so long that Gareth would find contentment with someone. His marriage to Anthea was so wretched. He deserves happiness. You both do."

"I fear his past marriage has left him with many scars," she confided. "I don't know everything that happened between the two of them, but I suspect it's going to take a great deal of time for your brother to lower his walls."

At her side, Hercules barked, as if in agreement.

She turned to the pug, realizing he had his eyes on her plate once again.

"More bacon?" she asked.

Hercules barked happily.

She tore off another small piece and held it out for him. "Only if you sit, my little gentleman."

He barked and sat, licking his chops. And then before she could drop the bacon, his eagerness had him rising to all fours again, performing an excited little dance of sorts on the Axminster.

She laughed, charmed by his canine enthusiasm. "Sit, Hercules."

He sat. She dropped the bacon, and he caught it in his mouth with a loud chomp.

How she wished her husband would be so easily tamed and won.

But she couldn't lead Gareth along with bacon. Was there something else she could use?

She took a sip of her coffee and looked at her sister-in-law across the table. "What was he like, before Anthea?"

"As the heir, he always had the weight of responsibility on him," Bette said. "But he was more lighthearted then. He used to enjoy reading and riding his horse. He loved boating and all manner of sport as well. He was exceptionally talented at cricket. He was the wicket-keeper."

It was almost impossible to imagine her staid, proper, icy husband involved in such lively antics. But she rather enjoyed the glimpse into the man he must have been once, before his marriage had left him jaded and reserved.

Could he be that man again?

As if he had heard her question, Hercules barked.

"Can you hear my thoughts, or are you hungry for more bacon?" she asked him.

At the mentioning of his new favorite dish, he gave another yip.

Lucy chuckled and offered him a bite. She was spoiling the hound and she knew it, but if she couldn't bring her husband to eat out of her hand, then she might as well settle for his adorable dog. Tending to the sweet pug certainly wasn't a hardship.

"So that's where you are."

At the sound of her husband's voice at her back, Lucy whirled in her chair. Hercules trotted happily to him, his tongue lolling, something resembling a lopsided smile on his furry face.

Solemnly, Gareth bent to give his dog a sound scratch behind his ears. The pug's curled tail wagged enthusiastically, and Lucy couldn't help but to think she knew the feeling too well. She, too, loved any hint of attention her husband bestowed upon her, however trifling. Good heavens, she was little better than the dog, content for a pat here or there, relegated to whatever bits of affection he chose to scatter in her direction. So like her relationship with her father.

The thought was sobering.

"I thought you had left for the day," Lucy told him.

After all, his tendency to disappear had become a daily affair. Each time she held out hope that something had changed and he'd lowered his walls, even the slightest bit, for her, she woke to breakfast with no one save Bette and Hercules for company yet again.

"Not today," her husband said mysteriously. "I'm in my study. Hercules was with me for a time, but when I looked at his bed, he was gone. I had a suspicion I might find him here with you. Mrs. Parr tells me you've been spoiling the scamp. Something about feeding him too much bacon."

Lucy bit her lip, certain her guilt was written on her face. "Only a few scraps here and there," she evaded.

Or three just now in rather hasty succession. But he didn't need to know that.

From the opposite end of the table, Bette was chortling into her tea, enjoying their tableau far too much.

"He's been getting rounder about the middle," Gareth

136

said, straightening to his full height again and staring down his nose at her.

For a wild moment, Lucy wondered what he would do if she scooped up a spoonful of poached egg and hurled it at him. Just like she'd done with Madeline when they'd been girls. Their food fights had been legendary until their nurse had grown tired of cleaning up after them and had complained to Mother, who had been quite horrified to know her daughters had been waging war in the nursery with aspics and pies and creams.

But she stifled that childish urge, leaving her spoon where it rested.

"Perhaps he is in need of more fresh air and restorative walks," she suggested brightly. "Has it ever occurred to you that he grows weary of being a prisoner within these walls?"

She was talking about herself every bit as much as Hercules, but she doubted Gareth knew it. Theirs was a customary aristocratic marriage, perfectly polite. It was only in the bedchamber that the manacles of propriety fell away. Or the carriage. Or the music room. Once, in the small walled gardens when no one else had been about. She had ridden him to her heart's content on a stone bench, and the next day, her knees had ached terribly.

It had been worth the pain.

"A prisoner," Gareth repeated, his hard, cold stare on her. Assessing. Seeing far too much. "Is that what you think he is?"

"How is he anything less?" she asked quietly.

Her words hung in the air, laden with meaning. Bette settled her dish of tea on the table with an unladylike rattle that reminded Lucy belatedly that she and Gareth had an audience aside from the gleefully unaware pug.

"Perhaps I should take him for a walk today, then," Gareth said. "Right now, in fact."

137

Hercules tilted his head at the word *walk*, which was clearly every bit as much a favorite as *bacon* was.

Lucy slanted a quick glance toward the windows. "Isn't it raining?"

"The more salient question might be, when is it not raining?" he quipped with a lightness that surprised her.

He wasn't wrong about that. The weather was always quite a bit different from what she had been accustomed to, but she'd also been spending so much time here at Claremont House that she often forgot to even take note.

"Does he like the rain?" she asked instead.

"Oh yes," Gareth told her. "He said that he does."

More lightness from him. A hint of levity, even. Had he been drinking brandy in his study again?

Her eyes narrowed on him. "I wasn't aware that you spoke dog."

"Only pug," he assured her. "Fluently, I might add."

Bette chuckled again from her side of the table.

"Well, since you speak his language and I don't, perhaps you should ask him if he would like me to accompany him on his walk," she suggested boldly, daring him to deny her.

To push her away and keep her at a safe distance as he had managed to do whenever they weren't tearing at each other's clothes. For only in lovemaking did he allow her close. Even then, however, he kept a part of himself from her. When they finished, he always withdrew. From her body, from her bed, from her room.

"He said he would be delighted," Gareth told her somberly.

Hardly an invitation. It had come from the dog instead of him. But Lucy was fool enough to accept it.

"I'll just change into a gown more suited to walking," she told him before turning back to her sister-in-law. "Bette, will you be joining us?"

"It's raining," she said. "I think I'll find a book to read."

And that sounded like a sensible plan to Lucy. But since she'd never been particularly rational herself, she rose from her chair and went in search of a promenade gown that wouldn't be ruined if it became wet.

By THE TIME Gareth descended from the carriage at Hyde Park, it was only misting. Which was fortunate since Hercules had never cared for rain, and it had been on his account that Gareth and Lucy had taken the brougham to the park. Hercules had never been particularly fond of carriage rides, but he had spent the duration of the short journey down St James Street and Piccadilly happily curled up in Lucy's lap.

With a jaundiced eye in their direction, Gareth had declared his beloved dog a traitor whose allegiance had been won with nothing more than crisply fried pork belly. Lucy had smiled, whispered something into his dog's ear, and been rewarded with a lick to her chin that had delighted her.

It was lowering, the ease with which Hercules had fallen beneath Lucy's spell. And nettling. Not the least of which because his pug wasn't the only victim of his wife's charms. Gareth was beginning to fear he was in danger of trotting at her hems, begging for her attention, as well.

He took the leash she offered him, holding tightly as Hercules leapt to the ground, lest he attempt to scamper away and into the ever-present danger of carriage wheels, and then offered his wife his hand.

Lucy alighted with the effortless grace he had come to expect from her. She moved fluidly, her sensual nature somehow even evident in the bold way she carried herself.

Such reassurance. He couldn't help but to admire her, something he'd been doing with alarming frequency of late.

She smiled, her full lips tilting upward and somehow rendering her even more lovely. "It's a beautiful day for a walk."

In truth, it was gray and murky. There was a chill in the air that denoted the presence of autumn. And a thick fog had begun to settle around them. How like her to find the best in the moment. Yet another of her maddening yet wonderful qualities.

"If one doesn't mind the fog, the chill, and the mist," he quipped, offering her his arm. "Shall we?"

"Yes, we shall." With a sunny smile, she settled her gloved hand in his proffered arm, and Hercules delightedly stretched himself to the end of his leash, leading the way.

"He seems to know where he's going," Lucy commented. "If I didn't know better, I would say you've taken him for walks before. And yet, how could that be when you're scarcely in residence?"

There was a pointed undercurrent in her words that he didn't miss.

He cleared his throat, keeping his attention focused on the pug shamelessly guiding them down the path. "I've been a trifle busy in recent weeks, but he and I often enjoyed morning walks here in the park."

"Why did you stop? Was it because of me?"

Yes. He couldn't very well linger and take Hercules for their customary walk when he had to escape his wife and all the unsettling ways she made him feel.

Gareth sighed. "Of course not, my dear."

"You're lying."

Her voice wasn't sharp, only slightly accusatory, and he was painfully aware of her regard. He turned to her, trying not to fall into her green eyes. Failing. Even in the gray paleness of the day, he could see the flecks of gold and cinnamon in their depths that never failed to enthrall him.

"Naturally some aspects of my daily routine have altered since our marriage," he said noncommittally and then promptly tripped over a stone, quite ruining the effect of his manufactured calm.

"Oh dear," Lucy exclaimed, her fingers tightening on his arm. "You nearly fell."

"I'm perfectly fine," he ground out, irritated with himself.

Irritated with her. Irritated with his damned traitorous pug.

Hercules glanced back at him in superior fashion, as if to crow *I have four legs to look after and still manage to walk with grace.*

"*Et tu, Brute?*" he muttered beneath his breath at his former best friend.

Hercules licked his nose and turned around, carrying on with his walk.

"It wasn't my intention to overset you," Lucy said quietly at his side as they continued.

Christ.

What must she think of him? Their marriage existed in the bedchamber alone, when he was free to surrender to the dark desire burning through him. He didn't know how the hell to be a husband by day. A husband to her.

He'd been one before, but his previous marriage had been vastly different from this one. It hadn't, he was beginning to realize, been a true marriage at all. He'd spent his years married to Anthea in a perpetual misery, unable to be the husband she needed while she gradually became an invalid increasingly dependent upon the laudanum that soothed her but ultimately had killed her. The notion of falling into that same trap of agony in his second marriage made him ill. He couldn't bear to endure it again. It was far preferable to feel nothing at all.

"You didn't overset me," he lied again for the sake of his pride. "It was a cursed pebble."

"Of course," Lucy said easily, allowing him the pretense. "Bette was telling me that you were excellent at playing cricket," she said then, quite surprising him, "amongst other manners of sport."

She had been speaking with his sister about him?

His brows drew together. "That was many years ago, when I was at Cambridge."

"What else did you like to do then?" she asked. "What made you happy?"

He tried to recall a time when his happiness had been the concern of anyone and couldn't seem to remember. "I'm not certain. It hardly matters now, does it? I'm a man of four-and-thirty with far too many responsibilities."

"Such as attending your club?" she asked archly.

Hercules stopped by a tree before them, lifted his leg, and proceeded to relieve himself on the trunk. They paused as one to allow the dog to mark his territory.

"Is that a note of chastisement I hear in your voice, my dear?" he asked, turning toward her again.

She was far more than lovely, his wife. She was beautiful. Being in her presence never failed to stir his blood. This morning, she was particularly stunning in a dashing hat and a navy promenade gown that hugged her enviable figure in all the right places.

She tilted her head at him, taking her time with her answer. "Merely a question. Isn't there anything you miss from your younger days? Some dream you've long since abandoned?"

Suddenly, he thought of his aspirations of poetry, an art he'd long since abandoned. It seemed terribly foolish now, the restless scribblings of a young man who hadn't an inkling of the ugliness awaiting him in life.

"I fancied myself a poet once," he found himself admitting as Hercules trotted away from the tree and they resumed their pace. "No longer, however."

"A poet," she repeated, seizing his arm in both hands. "You?"

Heat crept up his throat. "You think me incapable?"

"I think you're capable of far more than you think," she told him cryptically.

What the hell did that mean? He wanted to ask her, but he also wasn't certain he was ready to hear her answer. He was more than aware that his first marriage had left him as little more than a shell of the man he'd once been. But he didn't know how to ever be so youthful and idealistic and naïve any longer. All his hopes had been slowly robbed from him as the once-vibrant woman he'd married had withered away until the day she'd breathed her last.

And perhaps she'd taken a part of him with her.

A part he could never reclaim.

He decided to change the subject. "You spoke of abandoned dreams. Do you have any?"

After all, he was more than aware that Lucy hadn't wanted to marry him. She'd made that abundantly clear. She was likely drowning in regret over finding herself bound to him for the rest of her life. Gareth didn't blame her if she was.

"My cosmetics business," she said wistfully. "It was my dearest hope to persuade my father to allow me to use my inheritance to buy a factory and begin manufacturing my creams to be sold. I wanted to put his legacy to shame one day."

He wasn't surprised at her mettle. Gareth remembered their conversation the day he'd been attempting to persuade her of the necessity for their marriage. She'd alluded to the desire to own a business. But she hadn't been so specific. Now, he thought of the cream she'd offered him the day she'd shaved him, when she'd intruded upon his bedroom and his peace with such determination.

She never had brought it for him. He'd chased her away that morning, and every morning after, for he had locked the door between their chambers to keep her out.

He rubbed his free hand idly over his jaw now, recalling how intimate it had felt, her standing near in her dressing gown, gently dragging the razor over his skin. Attending him, as she had called it. He longed to have that intimacy again, with a sudden, astonishing force that made his teeth ache. Why had he been so determined to push her away, to send her fleeing to her bedchamber that morning? He ought to have kept her there. Allowed her to administer her cream and then shagged her silly.

"And now I've quite ruined your aspirations by making you my wife," he said, feeling grim.

By God, was it possible that he had destroyed his second wife's life just as surely as he had his first's? Neither had been his intention, but Gareth was beginning to wonder if there was something inherently wrong with him. If he possessed some invisible deficiency that rendered him poisonous to any woman who bound herself to him in holy matrimony.

"I'm more than aware that it isn't proper for a countess to dabble in trade," she said. "Even in our circles at home, it wasn't considered polite for a woman to start her own business. It's a sphere that is solely dedicated to men, while women are doomed to be the well-dressed, bejeweled decorations clinging to a gentleman's arm."

The irony of her assessment wasn't lost on him.

"Is that what you think of yourself?" he queried, turning back to her as Hercules found an intriguing patch of grass to investigate. "That you're nothing more than an ornamentation on my arm?"

"A broodmare as well," she said stubbornly. "Someone to share your bed and give you heirs."

Damn it. He didn't like the sound of that. Not one whit.

"And that is what you think of me, that all I want is for you to suffer my desires and bear me children?" he demanded.

Gareth kept his voice low, aware of the passersby around them. It wasn't the sort of discussion one ought to have in public, and yet he couldn't seem to help himself.

"I don't suffer them," she said. "You needn't fear that. Your first wife and I are nothing alike in that sense."

He knew that and was bloody glad of it. But she hadn't answered his question.

"Do you think I want nothing more from you than to give me heirs, to have no aspirations of your own?" he repeated.

"I'm not sure what I'm meant to think, Gareth," she returned, the cheerful smile she'd kept pinned to her lips from the moment they'd left the carriage fading for the first time. "You remain very much a stranger to me. I scarcely see you unless it's when you exercise your husbandly rights."

"Jesus," he gritted. "Don't call it that."

"What would you have me call it, then?" she countered. "Fornication? Making the beast with two backs? Engaging in sexual congress?"

A proper matron in black bombazine passed them, her expression properly scandalized.

"Lower your voice, madam," Gareth warned. "You'll cause a scene."

"We can't have a scene, can we?" Lucy's voice was bitter as she averted her gaze to Hercules, and they resumed walking. "It's far more comfortable to pretend we have no feelings at all, isn't it? That we have no emotions trapped inside, that we're nothing better than living blocks of ice doomed to pass each other in the night like ships."

"If you want to start a cosmetics business, you should do so," he told her hoarsely, meaning those words.

He didn't care if all London looked down their noses at them. He wanted, quite desperately, for Lucy to be content. He wanted to give her things he didn't know how to give her. But surely he could offer her that much—the freedom to pursue the dream she'd abandoned.

"I don't fool myself into believing my father ever would have allowed it," she said sadly. "Like Mother, he was quite intent upon settling me with an aristocratic husband. Not for my own sake, mind you, but for his. He thinks he'll be able to lord it over the upper ten thousand that his daughter has married an earl."

Gareth suddenly hated himself for the role he had unintentionally played in giving her parents what they so desperately wanted without a thought for what *she* had wanted. That hadn't been his intention. Everything between them had happened with such unprecedented swiftness, and the intensity of his reaction to her had been unlike anything he'd experienced previously. As a man who had been stripped of nearly everything in life he'd once valued, he had still placed heavy importance upon his sense of honor, and that had propelled him forward, with little thought for the rest.

"Your dowry is yours to do with as you please, Lucy," he said. "Start your cosmetics business with it. At Sherborne Manor, I became acquainted with Valentine Blakemoor, and the man is a property magnate. I'm certain he'd be willing to assist in helping you to find a factory where you might have your creams manufactured, particularly given your friendship with his wife, Lady Edith."

"It would be scandalous," Lucy told him needlessly. "Everyone would be gossiping about the dreadful American

Countess of Rexingham. We'd be turned away from polite society."

Would they? He wasn't so certain. And he also didn't think he cared. He had always kept a close circle of trusted friends. What need did he have of the rest? He's spent so much of his life mired in misery. Why should he allow the opinions of others to dictate his future or, for that matter, Lucy's?

"Society can go hang for all I care," he told her.

"This from the man who demanded I marry him for the sake of his honor," she quipped.

"My honor doesn't have a thing to do with Society," he explained. "It's a personal, private matter. What I did was wrong. My actions needed to be rectified."

"What a strange man you are," she said without heat. "I'm not sure I'll ever understand you."

Ha! She wasn't alone in that. Gareth didn't understand himself either.

"You have the rest of our lives to try," he said with a wry smile.

And then, he carried on down the path, following Hercules in his excited exploration of the park, a quiet, thoughtful Lucy at his side.

CHAPTER 11

"This is going to have a terrible ending, isn't it?" Lucy asked Gareth from the haven of their private box at Her Majesty's Theatre.

The second act of *Lucia di Lammermoor* had just begun, but Lucy already had a knot of dread coiled in her belly, because poor Lucia had just been handed a forged letter telling her that the man she loved had thrown her over for another woman.

"It is a tragedy, my dear," her husband said calmly at her side. "I do believe it's a requirement for the ending to be terrible."

She sighed, watching as Lucia wept into the letter as her scheming brother Enrico watched from the periphery, apparently unmoved by his machinations and his sister's pain.

"The poor woman ought to find the nearest sword and run her scoundrel brother through," Lucy said. "Or better yet, find a pistol and shoot him. It would spare her so much heartache if she only realized he's betraying her."

"My," Gareth drawled. "Americans are a bloodthirsty lot, aren't they?"

It wasn't the first time she'd heard such an observation.

"We are when we need to be," she countered, unabashed.

"I've begun to discover you're quite intimidating when you choose to be," he said, keeping his gaze trained on the stage below.

What a strange thing to say to her. Lucy wondered what he meant by it. How could it be possible that *she* could intimidate *him*? His frigid air and his closed-off manner, the insurmountable walls he'd built around himself, his aloof disinterest in anything other than the passion they shared—that was the true definition of intimidating. But Lucy held her tongue.

She studied his handsome profile for a moment longer than necessary before returning her attention to the stage where Lucia and Enrico were singing beautifully together. Sitting in an opera box with Gareth was the last place she had imagined to find herself this evening. But following their morning walk with Hercules, her husband's demeanor had subtly changed. He had left for his customary afternoon diversions, only to return early, bearing tickets for the opera and requesting that she join him.

They had dined with Bette and then departed in their evening finery for the opera house on the corner of Haymarket and Pall Mall. It was the most time she'd spent in her husband's presence since their wedding day, and Lucy had to admit, she enjoyed his company. He had been unusually attentive all evening, complimenting her on her gown and the ruby-and-diamond earrings and matching necklace she'd chosen for the occasion.

It felt, as she sat by his side and watched the drama unfolding before them, as if they were truly husband and wife instead of two strangers who were hopelessly attracted to each other. It felt almost as if their marriage was real and not the unfortunate product of the scandal they'd caused at Sherborne Manor.

The drama continued to unfold on the stage below, poor Lucia being shepherded into a marriage she didn't want with Arturo. Lucy held her breath as Lucia signed the marriage contract, her heart breaking, for she knew what was about to come next. Edgardo rushed in, too late to save the woman he loved from marrying another.

"Oh no," Lucy murmured, pressing a hand over her lips.

"Take heart, my dear," Gareth drawled at her side. "It's only an opera."

She knew that, of course. But the plight of Lucia and Edgardo filled her with sadness just the same.

"Yes, but how does it end?" she asked. "I've never seen this one before, and I have a dreadful feeling it's only going to get worse for the two of them."

"Act Three is rather fond of gore," he said mildly.

Lucy shook her head, trying to understand him. "And it doesn't affect you at all?"

"The characters aren't real," he explained. "Life itself is far harsher than an opera could ever be."

His life had been, she thought. But he still refused to share that part of himself with her—the part that had been so badly, cruelly hurt. He hadn't always been the man he was now. His heart was battered and scarred.

"Why did you bring me here tonight?" she asked softly.

His countenance remained impassive. "I thought you would enjoy it."

"That was considerate of you."

He flashed her a mocking smile. "I'm not entirely an ogre, Lucy."

And suddenly, her heart was no longer aching for the fictional characters on the stage, but for him. For the proud, handsome man she'd married. The man whose previous marriage had left him cold and distant. The man whose desire had brought her to life, whose kisses moved her more than any she'd ever experienced.

The man she had fallen in love with.

The notion made her breath catch. She hadn't intended to lose her heart to Gareth, but it had happened nonetheless.

"I never thought you were an ogre," she told him firmly, turning her mind to their conversation instead of the unsettling realizations flitting through.

He raised a dark brow. "Even though I forced you into marrying me?"

"It could be argued that we forced each other. I kissed you back, after all."

"Yes, you did." His stare darkened, glittering with sensual intent. "I must admit, I find myself increasingly glad you mistook me for the butler."

"It was the footman," she corrected, although she was certain he was getting the servant's position wrong intentionally. "And I'm glad I mistook you for him as well."

"You are?" There was a faint note of something in his voice that she couldn't define.

Hope? Surely not. Surely that was her own fanciful nature thinking she'd heard something she hadn't.

"I am," she affirmed just the same.

And then the curtains closed on the second act, and Gareth shot from his seat as if it had suddenly caught flame.

"I'll fetch you a refreshment, my dear," he said.

Before she could offer a protest, he was gone.

As had become customary over the course of their marriage, Gareth knocked at the door between his chamber and Lucy's.

And as was also customary, she bade him enter. He hesitated just a moment before opening the portal and joining her, a strange new heaviness in his chest that had somehow lodged itself there over the course of the day.

But the lust that had been burning hot and bright inside him ever since he had taken one look at her in her elegant red evening gown remained insistent, spurring him on against any misgivings. He opened the door to find her seated before her mirror, her mahogany hair unbound, a silver brush sweeping carefully through the strands. She smiled at him over her shoulder in welcome, and it shouldn't have been sultry, shouldn't have made his prick rise to attention, the simple gesture. And yet it was and it did.

"Hullo," she said softly.

"Good evening," he returned, stiffly formal.

Despite the weeks that had passed, he was still painfully unfamiliar with a wife who welcomed him into her chamber, into her bed. He couldn't shake the notion that she was like a butterfly, and that if he made any sudden moves, she might flit away into the sky, never to return. His inability to be a proper husband to her frustrated him.

Likely, he would make Lucy miserable eventually. The brilliance in her eyes would diminish just as Anthea's had done. She would look at him with shadows and sadness in her emerald gaze. He would be a disappointment, just as he had been before.

"I was just brushing my hair for the evening while I awaited you," Lucy said brightly.

"Allow me," he said, crossing the chamber to her and reaching for the ornate handle of the brush.

She relinquished it, her expression one of surprise. "Thank you."

He inclined his head, meeting her gaze in the mirror as he

ran the brush through her silken hair. "You shaved me. It's only fair that I return the favor somehow."

Lucy smiled, then bit her lip.

Gareth stilled. "Did I hurt you?"

"Not at all," she reassured him.

He resumed brushing. "What troubled you, then?"

"I was only thinking of your displeasure with me that day for my intrusion and wondering…" Her words trailed away.

"Wondering what?" he prodded.

"It doesn't matter."

"It matters to me."

They engaged in a staring match in the mirror, until she finally relented with a small sigh. "I was wondering if it would ever be different between us. If you would ever look at me with welcome when I knock at your door instead of looking at me as if I'm an intruder who doesn't belong here. If you would ever leave it unlocked in the morning."

Hell.

Gareth's fingers tightened on the handle of the brush, the decorations adorning it cutting into his skin. "Of course you belong here. You're my wife."

"It hasn't felt that way," she said quietly.

He knew he was to blame for that, and he hated the hurt lacing her voice. Hated knowing he was the cause of it. It seemed he was doomed to repeat the mistakes of his past.

Gareth placed the brush on the tray before her where her lady's maid had assembled her toilette. "Perhaps I should leave you to your rest this evening."

"Is that your answer to unhappiness?" Lucy asked sharply. "To simply retreat and pretend as if it doesn't exist? If that is what you did with your first wife, little wonder your marriage was so miserable."

He stared at her reflection, everything within him seizing. She wasn't wrong. He had been retreating from her ever

153

since their wedding day. It hadn't occurred to him that it had been what he had done with Anthea as well, albeit for different reasons. Separating himself had been necessary because she'd been withering away, and the greater her sickness became, the stronger her hatred and resentment of Gareth. He had despised seeing her in her sickroom, propped up by pillows, gaunt and pale, refusing to permit anyone to open the curtains or the windows and allow in light and fresh air. She'd been dying slowly, and he had seen it, had known it, and yet he'd been helpless to do anything to stop it.

"Gareth," Lucy said, rising from her chair and whirling to face him. "I didn't mean that."

"I rather think you did," he said, amazed at the calmness of his voice, given the riot inside him.

God, what a muddle he'd made of everything. Lucy deserved better.

"Forgive me," she entreated, reaching for him. "Please."

"I don't have much gentleness in me at the moment, Lucy," he warned.

Her hand settled on his forearm anyway, her touch light and yet searing him through his shirt sleeve. "I'm not sure you ever had gentleness in you. Stay, please. Don't go. Don't leave me alone tonight."

He shouldn't listen to her, and he knew it. There was something brutal rising within him. Something feral and raw and overwhelming. It was more than desire. More than his regrets over the past and present. It was a conflagration threatening to burn him alive.

"You don't want me to stay," he rasped. "Not like this. It's better if I go."

"You're always walking away from me, Gareth." Her fingers tensed on his arm, as if she thought she might hold him there in her bedroom by force. "Stay with me."

Her eyes were pleading, her tone entreating. And he

wanted to surrender. To give in and stay with her, to make love to her all night long and selfishly lose himself in her body. But he would hate himself for that more than he already did.

"You're asking me for something I can't give you. I can't be the husband you deserve, the man who is worthy of you. I'm too damned broken from the past."

"I don't believe that," she said stubbornly. "The man you were once is still inside you. The brother Bette remembers is there, waiting for you to find him and set him free."

She made it sound so easy. But it wasn't. No one knew that better than Gareth. He'd spent years trapped in a hellacious marriage, and he still bore all the scars to prove it. Damn her for thinking she could sweep in here with her optimism and her cheer and her sensual allure. For believing she could somehow make him whole again when he knew bloody well she couldn't.

"You're overstepping," he snapped coolly. "This is a marriage of convenience, nothing more. I'm not some stray mongrel for you to collect and attempt to feed and bathe, for Christ's sake."

She flinched as if he had struck her, and he regretted the venom in his words, made sharp by so many ugly memories he couldn't seem to forget, no matter how hard he tried.

"Of course it is," she said, her tone wooden, her countenance lacking its customary vibrancy. "Forgive me for going too far."

The devil of it was, he wanted her still. He selfishly, foolishly wanted her. He wanted to strip her out of her dressing gown, lay her on the bed, and bury his cock deep inside her. He wanted to use her to forget as he had so many times. To become mindless from the pleasure she gave him, the pleasure he'd been so long denied in his first marriage.

But he needed to remind himself that happiness was a

chimera, forever out of reach. His American spitfire would one day come to hate him. She would regret their marriage, lose interest in him, find another lover to fill her bed. It was only a matter of time.

It had been a mistake to spend so much time with her today. He could see that now. He'd given her false hope where none should dwell.

"I married you because I had no other choice," he said, forcing himself to be cruel. "You'd do best to remember it."

Her chin went up in stubborn defiance, but he didn't miss her sudden pallor. "Of course, my lord. How could I forget? I threw myself at you like the wanton hoyden I am, and you had no choice but to save my reputation with your benevolence."

Her tone, like her words, was as sharp as a blade.

He continued anyway, desperate to put some distance between them, to make her see the futility in her optimism.

"It is a duty I bear in the name of my title," he said coldly. "After you give me children, you'll be free to pursue life as you wish without me to weigh you down. I expect you shall be far more content then."

"Are you suggesting that I should take lovers after I've given you your heir?" she asked, sounding hurt.

He inclined his head. "The practice is quite customary in aristocratic marriages."

"And is that how your last marriage was conducted?"

"No," he bit out. "Anthea never gave me an heir, as you know."

He had tried at the beginning of their marriage. But Anthea had been far more interested in opium than him. Throughout the course of their marriage, that had never changed, although many other things had.

"Perhaps I should lie on the bed now and let you have your way with me so that we can both carry on with this marriage of convenience and forget it ever happened," Lucy suggested acidly. "The sooner you get your broodmare pregnant, the better."

It was the second time she had referred to herself thusly in the span of one day. He hadn't liked it the first time, and he most certainly didn't like it now. Even if he was responsible for her feeling that way. It was necessary, he told himself. The sooner she accepted the truth of their union, the better it would be for the both of them.

Just look at how dreadfully awry today had gone. He'd caused her pain. He would only cause her more.

"Don't call yourself that," he said curtly.

"Why shouldn't I?" Her elegant fingers moved to the buttons fastening her dressing gown, plucking one free of its moorings, then another. "That is what I am meant to be. This is a marriage of convenience, one you very much regret entering, and one you've made more than clear exists for one reason alone." More buttons came undone.

She was furious with him, he realized, twin patches of pink on her high cheekbones. She looked nothing short of glorious, like a vengeful goddess descended among mortals to wreak havoc upon men. Upon him, specifically. He should have been satisfied that he'd rebuilt the crumbling wall between them. He should be returning to his chamber, leaving her to stew in her outrage.

But he was transfixed by the sight of her undoing those blasted buttons. He couldn't move. Couldn't breathe. Longing slammed into him with the force of a locomotive. Not just for her body, but for *her*. For her tenderness, her smiles, her laughter, her cheer, her undying persistence. For everything that was Lucy. It was bigger than he was, sudden and intense. Terrifying. He tamped it down, banishing the unwanted emotions.

"This isn't what I intended tonight," he said thickly.

"Then what did you intend, Gareth? To crush my heart beneath your heel with your callousness? If so, you've succeeded." Her fingers were trembling, he realized, and she paused on a button that was stubbornly refusing to be freed.

With a feminine howl of pure frustration, she tore at the remaining buttons, sending them raining over the carpets in dull thuds, rolling across the floor like tiny pearl recriminations. She was naked under that blasted *robe de chambre*. Naked and beautiful. Her full, luscious breasts, the nip of her waist, her lush hips, the curve of her legs, her creamy throat, and hard nipples all on display.

She held out her hands, unashamed. "Here I am. Take me."

"Not like this," he growled, belatedly recalling her words.

Her heart? What did that mean? He wasn't sure he wanted to know.

She reached for him, took one of his hands in hers, thrust it crudely between her legs. "This is what you want, isn't it? Only this and nothing more. Have it, then. Have it and be gone."

To his shame, he allowed his hand to linger for longer than he should have, spurred by the sleek heat of her sex. She was wet. Even in her anger, she wanted him, and the knowledge made him long to do everything she demanded. To bend her over the bed and sink his cock inside her. To take her roughly from behind. To cup her breasts as he fucked her, pinch her nipples and bite her shoulder. To do everything that kept him awake at night, long into the hours of darkness.

Damn it, no.

He came to his senses, withdrawing from her. "You're overset. Get some rest, my dear. I'll see you in the morning."

With great difficulty, and summoning every speck of restraint he possessed, Gareth turned away from her, leaving her there, alone and naked and angry, his vengeful American goddess. The wife he hadn't wanted, and yet, the wife he couldn't seem to get enough of. The door had scarcely closed at his back before he heard a frustrated cry from her bedchamber and the undeniable thud of some poor inanimate object striking it.

CHAPTER 12

"*All* the gowns, Lady Rexingham?"

Lucy pinned a false smile to her lips for the sake of her lady's maid. "I wish you wouldn't call me that. Do you think you might call me Lucy instead?"

The sweet-natured English lady's maid she had hired to replace her American maid blinked at her, looking horrified. "It wouldn't be proper, my lady."

Lucy sighed. Of course it wouldn't be proper. Even if she didn't feel like a true wife, she was the Countess of Rexingham for better or for worse, for richer or for poorer, et cetera. Well, she might have Gareth's title, but he could take his marriage of convenience and his frigid, heartless self and the walls he built, and he could stuff them in his ear.

"All the gowns," she told her lady's maid. "Please see that everything that belongs to me is packed and delivered to Mrs. Chartrand at Number Eight, Lark Square. I'll take a trunk with me this morning, but anything that doesn't fit in the carriage will have to follow. I'll send my mother's carriage to fetch the rest."

"Everything, my lady?" the lady's maid repeated hesitantly.

"Yes," she said firmly. "Everything."

Because after Gareth had left her last night, she had crawled miserably into her lonely bed and cried herself to sleep. But before slumber had claimed her, she had made a decision.

She was leaving him. She didn't know all the particulars of marriage law, but she was reasonably certain she could obtain a divorce. If not in England, then at home in New York City. It was simple.

Her husband didn't want her.

He didn't love her.

Gareth had made it clear on numerous occasions, but she had been too stubborn and foolish to listen. But when he had walked away from her instead of staying—instead of fighting with her, fighting *for* her—she had known she couldn't continue ignoring the truth. She had fallen in love with an icy man who was incapable of caring for her in return. And if she remained here, he would only continue crushing her heart. Day by day, minute by minute, hour by hour, until eventually nothing would remain.

"As you wish, Lady Rexingham," her lady's maid said, sounding subdued.

"Thank you," Lucy said, a quaver in her voice.

But she would not cry. She had wept enough tears last night. Today, she had vowed, she would be strong. Strong enough to get to her mother's town house before she humiliated herself, that was.

She had lingered here enough where she wasn't welcome. It was time to go. With a deep, fortifying breath, Lucy took her leave of the bedroom that had never quite managed to feel like her own. She had made a few changes, adding pictures, some of her own *objets d'art*. But she'd never felt as if she belonged there. The room, like her husband's heart, wasn't hers, and it never would be.

Clenching her jaw against a stinging rush of tears that threatened to fall, she descended the curved staircase she had traversed without thought so many times before. This time felt different, knowing it would be her last. Her heart ached at the thought of never seeing Gareth again. Never touching him, kissing him, never being held in his arms. But the choice had been his, and he had made it with cruel finality. How she would miss him and Bette and Hercules, too. Her little life here at Claremont House had begun to feel comfortable.

Too comfortable, likely. Perhaps she just wasn't meant for happiness. Or perhaps she was meant to start her cosmetics business just as she had longed to do.

She reached the bottom of the stairs to find her sister-in-law bustling toward her, a worried expression on her lovely face.

"Good morning, Bette," Lucy said, trying to keep her voice from trembling.

"Good morning," Bette greeted, frowning. "Hercules and I missed you at breakfast."

The sweet pup. His enthusiasm for the most mundane activities was an endless source of delight for her. If only she could take him with her. Tears pricked at her eyes, and she blinked furiously, banishing them before they could fall.

"I hope you gave him some bacon for me," she said, hating herself for the way her voice broke on the last word.

"Is something amiss?" Bette asked, her gaze searching. "Mrs. Parr said that your trunks are being packed."

Of course the housekeeper would have been notified of Lucy's requests. She should have thought of that.

"I'm leaving," she told her sister-in-law.

"Leaving London?"

"Leaving your brother," she elaborated gently. "I find I can no longer remain here. I'm going to my mother's town house this morning and, from there, back to New York City as soon as I'm able to secure passage."

"Oh, Lucy, no," Bette lamented. "What has happened between the two of you? Yesterday, you seemed so happy. I was beginning to have hopes for you both. Was it the opera? I told Gareth he shouldn't take you to see that dreadful *Lucia di Lammermoor*. It's not romantic in the slightest. Everyone dies."

Not everyone had died, but Lucia and her Edgardo had. It was rather symbolic, Lucy thought grimly.

"It wasn't the opera." She patted her sister-in-law's arm, trying to console her. "It's your brother, I'm afraid. He's too unwilling to let go of the past, and I have no intention of spending the rest of my life in misery with him."

She loved him far too much to remain here, knowing he would never return that love. That he was either incapable of loving her or unwilling to try. But she kept that to herself, for it was too painful, too private. She'd come dangerously close to confessing her feelings to Gareth last night, and he had ignored it, just as if she hadn't said a word about her heart.

"But your marriage is so young," Bette protested. "Surely all you need is more time to get to know each other."

"He's made me realize that no amount of time will change anything," Lucy said sadly. "His heart is a closed and locked door, and he's thrown away the key."

"He cares for you, Lucy. I know that he does. This is the first time I've seen him happy since before he married Anthea."

"He doesn't care enough," she explained, another hitch in her voice that she couldn't contain. She was going to burst into tears at any moment. "I'll always remember you fondly, Bette. I do hope you'll write. Please take good care of

Hercules for me—extra bacon every morning. And please also take care of your brother."

She swallowed hard against a lump rising in her throat.

"He wouldn't want you to leave," her sister-in-law said, clutching at her arm. "Please, Lucy."

"Has he left for the morning already?" she asked, already knowing the answer.

"He has," Bette confirmed. "But he will return soon."

She gave her sister-in-law a brittle smile. "When he returns, I'll be gone. Where is Hercules? I'd like to bid him farewell before I go."

"On his bed in Gareth's study, I believe." Tears shone in Bette's eyes. "He'll miss you."

She had no doubt the loveable pup would. If only her husband felt the same.

Lucy gave her sister-in-law's arm a fond squeeze. "Take care of yourself, Bette."

She went to Gareth's study then, finding the door ajar, Hercules happily sleeping curled up on his bed. He opened his eyes drowsily as she approached, then yawned and rolled onto his back, requesting a belly rub. With a smile, she bent down and obliged.

"You're a very good boy, Hercules," she told him. "I'll miss you." Now a tear did slide free, traveling along the bridge of her nose to splash on the pug's belly. She sniffed. "Be good to your papa for me."

Hercules yawned again, then made a happy snuffling sound and closed his eyes.

She supposed that was his answer.

Holding back the torrent of tears that threatened to fall, she left her husband's study for the last time.

~

GARETH RETURNED to a house in turmoil.

He'd scarcely taken off his hat and coat when a distraught Bette nearly barreled into him, Hercules trotting at her heels.

"Is something wrong?" he asked, frowning.

He had awoken in a grim mood following his row with Lucy the night before. Determined to make amends with her, he had set out after an early breakfast for a meeting with Valentine Blakemoor to discuss properties he might lease for Lucy's cosmetics business. Not because he was feeling guilty about his poor treatment of her—although, in truth, he was. But rather, because he wanted to make her happy. There was no reason she should be robbed of her aspirations for the sin of becoming his wife.

"Lucy is gone," his sister told him, sniffling.

Belatedly, he realized her eyes were red-rimmed and puffy, the whites bloodshot. She had been weeping. And copious amounts, if her appearance was any indication. Something seized inside his chest.

"What do you mean, she's gone?"

"She l-left this morning," Bette said with a sob. "She's taken all her belongings with her. Every last stitch of clothing, all her perfumes and jewelry. There's nothing left. She told me she's returning to New York City as soon as she's able. That she is leaving you."

Jesus.

Gareth stood there in the marble entry of Claremont House where he had so many times before, painfully aware of the servants presiding over what should have been a private moment. A private conversation.

His wife was leaving him.

Had left him already.

God.

"Gar?" Bette said.

Hercules began sniffing Gareth's boots, then his trousers. And still, he stood, unmoving.

"What are you going to do?" his sister asked.

That was an excellent question. He didn't have the slightest notion other than that he couldn't do nothing. He had to do something. He…needed Lucy.

The realization made an odd, warm rush trickle through his chest.

Something that hadn't been there before. Or if it had, he hadn't been willing to acknowledge it. To allow himself to feel it. But it was there now.

She couldn't leave him. She was his wife, damn it. But it was his fault, and he knew it. He had treated her wretchedly last night. Had pushed her and pushed her until he'd finally pushed her too far.

"Did she tell you where she was going?" he asked hoarsely.

"To her mother's town house at Lark Square," Bette said. "You're going to go after her, aren't you, Gar? You're not going to just let her go, are you?"

He was a thick-witted fool, but he also knew when he had been wrong. And he had been wrong in the way he had treated Lucy. Wrong to think he could continue to keep walls between them and keep *her*.

And she was what mattered most. More than the ghosts of the past, more than old hurts and scars. More than anything and anyone else. That feeling inside him was growing bigger, stronger. He didn't just need Lucy.

He loved her.

He didn't know when it had happened, or why he'd been fighting it for so long, but he could acknowledge it now, for the first time. That sensation in his chest had a name. The heart he'd thought long incapable of finer emotion was beating for her alone.

"Gar? You're going to go to her, aren't you?" Bette prodded.

Hercules nudged his boot, almost as if exhorting him to move.

"I am," he confirmed, knowing he had no other option.

If he didn't go after Lucy now, he would lose her forever.

Gareth turned to his butler, who was hovering nearby, attempting to act as if he hadn't overheard the conversation. "Have my carriage brought round again, if you please." Reaching down, he patted his beloved pug on the head. "I'm going to fetch her, lad. Don't worry."

CHAPTER 13

"You can't divorce the earl," Mother said, looking aghast. "You've only just married him."

Lucy should have known her mother wouldn't be pleased to return from her social jaunts to discover that her daughter had once more installed herself in the Lark Square town house where she'd spent much of her time in England.

"I married him over a month ago," Lucy corrected, holding her head high and doing her best not to start weeping again.

"Scarcely any time at all," her mother snapped, frowning.

"Enough time for me to know that I don't want to spend the rest of my life with a man who is incapable of loving me," she corrected.

They were seated in the formal sitting room that her mother had often reserved for guests. But then, Lucy supposed, the chamber choice had likely been Mother's way of reminding her that she was a guest here, no longer a resident. If only Madeline were here instead of off with her own husband. Her beloved sister would have given their mother

168

an earful on her behalf, she knew. But Madeline was in love and deliriously happy, which was precisely what she deserved, even if Lucy was bitter that such marital bliss had eluded her.

"Do you have any idea of the scandal it will cause back in New York if word were to spread that you have deserted the Earl of Rexingham after only one month of marriage?" Mother asked. "I'll never again be able to show my face in society. To say nothing of how furious your father will be. He spent a fortune on making every detail of your wedding perfect."

"Perfect for *you*," she couldn't help pointing out. "I didn't want a cake that required a small army to bake and assemble or Brussels lace or a Worth gown or myrtle flowers or a diamond tiara. That was what you wanted. Just as marrying the earl was what *you* wanted."

Her mother's nostrils flared in a rare show of temper— Mother considered it dreadfully impolite to show any hint of true anger. "Have you forgotten that your own reckless actions prompted your marriage? I'll not be blamed for your hoyden ways. If you are unhappy with the earl, you might have thought about it before you threw yourself into his arms and…and did whatever else it was that the Marchioness of Featherstone saw you doing."

"Kissing him, Mother," she couldn't resist elaborating. "I was kissing him."

"Good heavens, I was trying to spare us both the shame of saying it aloud," her mother said with a delicate shudder. "You mustn't speak of it again. But it bears repeating that you should have considered what you were doing very carefully before doing it. Now you have to live with your decisions."

"I'm not going back to him," she denied vehemently. "He's made it more than clear that we have nothing more than a marriage of convenience and that I mean nothing to him. I'm a means to an end. He married me to satisfy his honor, but all he wants is his heir and spare."

"That is how these things are done, my dear," Mother told her. "It's so much more civil than most marriages. I had five children before your father was gracious enough to take his attentions elsewhere."

Lucy had two other siblings who had been born after her, one a boy and the other a girl. Neither of them had survived infancy, William Jr. dying shortly after birth and Phoebe claimed by a fever just short of her first birthday. Their losses were a part of her, and she would forever mourn them. This was the first time she'd ever heard her mother speak of all her siblings in such a manner. And it was certainly the first time she had heard her mother speak of her intimate relationship with her father.

"Are you saying Father has a mistress?" she asked, feeling vaguely ill.

"I'm saying it isn't my concern," her mother said brightly. "Mr. Chartrand is content to conduct his affairs as he pleases, and I am content to do the same. It's why I've chosen to remain in London while he returned to New York City."

Lucy had foolishly supposed the reason had been the marriages her daughters had made. Now, she saw her mother clearly for possibly the first time, and she didn't like the picture before her.

"That isn't the sort of marriage I want for myself," she said quietly.

She loved Gareth. Loved him enough to leave him. Because if she didn't, her love for him would ultimately destroy her.

"It isn't always our decision, the sort of marriage we have," her mother returned sternly. "You've married the earl, and you must accept it. You can't stay here. I'll not shelter you from your husband. You belong at his side, in his home."

Defeat washed over her. "Don't you see? I don't belong there. I never did. All I need is a roof over my head until I can arrange for passage back to New York City. Then, I'll be gone, and you'll never need to worry about me again."

"You make me sound heartless, my dear. I'm only acting in your best interest."

"Are you?" Lucy rose to her feet, fury making her incapable of remaining seated. "Or are you acting in your own best interest? Because I must say that it seems the latter is what you've been doing for my whole life. You knew neither Madeline nor I wanted to marry an English aristocrat. Coming to England was your dream, not ours. Entering this society, my marrying an earl, it was what you wanted."

"All I have ever wanted is what's best for you, Lucy," her mother said, her lower lip quivering as if she were going to burst into tears. "How dare you suggest otherwise? I've been a wonderful mother to you. You've had only the best of everything."

Except her mother's love.

Lucy didn't say that, however.

"If you won't allow me to stay with you, then I'll take a room at a hotel," she told her mother. "I'm not going to stay in an unhappy marriage just to spare you the shame in your social circle. I deserve better."

Head held high, Lucy swept from the room. She didn't make it far before she realized she had dismissed the coachman, sending him and the landau back to Claremont House. Which meant she was going to have to beg her mother for the use of her carriage.

That rather ruined the effect of her grand exit, she thought grimly, still quivering with outrage. She would simply walk to a hotel. It was only noon. She had plenty of daylight to guide her, and the leaden skies had yet to deliver the promised rain. With any luck, she wouldn't even be wet. She could send a porter at the hotel for her trunks.

Lucy retrieved her wrap and other effects before leaving her mother's town house. The wind possessed a slight chill, but she would find warmth if she kept moving. Determined, she proceeded down the pavements, trying her utmost to keep her composure. The day had decidedly not gone as she had hoped it would.

Surely it would get better.

Caught up in her misery, she didn't recognize the landau until it drew alongside her and slowed. The door flew open, and Gareth leapt out.

"Lucy!"

She stopped, heart thudding. She hadn't expected him to even notice she had gone until he returned that evening from wherever he had been.

But he was here now, standing on the pavements before her, looking unfairly handsome.

"What are you doing here?" she asked sharply, afraid she would cry and truly humiliate herself.

"Bette told me you were going to your mother's," he explained, his blue gaze roving over her face. "That you've left me."

The raw hurt in his voice was new. She was accustomed to icy self-possession from him. But she refused to allow herself to hope for any emotion from him other than anger.

"You made yourself clear last night," she told him evenly, holding his gaze without flinching. "I made the only decision left to me."

"What the devil are you doing on the street?"

Heat crept up her neck. "My mother refused to offer me shelter until I can book passage back to New York City. I decided to walk to the nearest hotel."

"No," he bit out.

"Yes," she countered.

"No, you're not walking to a hotel, and no, you're not leaving me." He took her arm in a firm but gentle hold, staying her when she would have continued.

Exasperation rose. "Yes, Gareth, I am."

"Come inside the carriage with me," he said, his voice gentling, losing some of its severity. "Please," he added when she remained stubbornly planted on the pavements, refusing to do what he wanted.

"Why?" she demanded, searching his countenance for some hint of what he was feeling. "Give me one reason that I should go anywhere with you."

"Because you're my wife," he told her steadily. "And because if you don't come with me, I'll get down on my knees in the midst of Lark Square and make a complete arse of myself by begging you."

He would beg?

No. What was she thinking?

She shook her head. "Those reasons aren't good enough."

"Because I can't lose you, damn it," he blurted. "You're the one bit of sunshine in my life aside from my damned hound and my sister. I swore I'd never marry again after Anthea, but then you threw yourself into my arms in a moonlit garden, and you managed to chase the darkness away. You made me see the light again. You're altogether wrong for me. You're a brazen American who somehow has the skills of a pick-pocket and the mouth of a sailor on the docks. You're bold and sensual and scandalous, and you are kind to my sister and endlessly patient with me, and even my dog likes you more than he likes me."

His voice was hoarse with pure emotion by the time he reached the end of his soliloquy. Even the customary mask of indifference he wore had slipped to reveal the true man beneath. And what she saw made hope swell inside her for the first time that day.

"That's probably because of all the bacon I give him," she said, her eyes going misty.

"It's because you're *you*, Lucy," Gareth said. "Because you're like the brightest star in the night sky, twinkling and gleaming, more brilliant than all the rest. Because when anyone comes to know you, they can't help but love you for everything you are. Bette loves you. Hercules loves you." He hesitated, catching her gloved hand in his before continuing. "*I* love you."

Lucy swayed on her feet, a sudden rush of tears making her vision blurry. She blinked, clearing them, convinced she'd misheard. Gareth, her Gareth who was always unbendingly stoic and icy, stood before her, looking at her with so much tenderness, such unfettered adoration, that for a moment, she couldn't speak. Couldn't think.

"Do you mean it?" she whispered, holding her breath as she waited for the answer.

"More than anything," he told her, kissing her hand. "I'm sorry it took me so long to realize what's been clear the moment your lips first touched mine—I'm yours. My heart belongs to you. I don't want a marriage of convenience or a broodmare. I want you, my wild, beautiful firebrand. I want your love, your companionship, your kisses, your touch, your everything. I know I don't deserve it. I don't deserve *you*. But I promise you that I'll do all that I can to earn your love. To earn having you at my side."

She squeezed his hand, overcome with emotion, and that was when the sky finally unleashed its vengeance, a sudden deluge pouring down on them. It was cold and pelting, but she didn't care. Didn't care that carriages were passing by them, curious stares peering out the windows. Didn't care that the wind stirred up, whipping at her skirts and making her shiver, that the rain pouring down her face was mingling with her tears.

Because this time, the tears she was shedding were tears of happiness instead of sorrow.

"Tell me again," she begged. "That you love me, I mean."

"I love you, Lucy," he said without hesitation, the rain lashing at his handsome face and soaking his hat and coat.

But he stood there with her, holding her, looking at her with so much love that neither the cold rain nor the the potential for scandal mattered. Gareth loved her. He loved her so much that he had finally made himself vulnerable, had at last allowed himself to feel. His ice had melted. The walls he'd erected around his heart had crumbled at last.

And he was hers. The past couldn't hurt them any longer. Her future awaited her, and it wasn't in New York City. It was here in London with the man she'd accidentally kissed one night in the gardens.

The best mistake she'd ever made.

"Good," she said simply. "Because I love you too. Now let's get out of the rain and go home where we belong."

EPILOGUE

*L*ucy, Countess of Rexingham, had possessed a great deal of good fortune in her life, but at the moment, standing in the marble entry hall of Claremont House, she was most concerned with her best bit of good luck: her husband and her daughter and, at their feet, Hercules.

Fanny clapped her pudgy hands delightedly from her perch in Gareth's arms. "Mama!" she cried with the sweet exuberance of a small child.

Hercules trotted happily toward her, his nails clicking on the marble floor in a familiar and beloved rhythm.

"Darling," her husband greeted, smiling at her in welcome, his countenance so much softer and relaxed than it had once been. "How was your meeting with Mr. Bellingham?"

"I'm pleased to say that he has decided to begin selling my cream in his department store," she announced, grinning and unable to contain her excitement.

She was thrilled that the owner of Bellingham and Co., one of London's oldest and most prestigious department stores, had agreed to offer her cream in their fragrance and toiletries department. He had also settled upon a selection of brushes, soaps, and fragrances her cosmetics company manufactured. In the two years since her marriage to Gareth, Lucy's fledgling business had grown with a haste that had surpassed her every hope.

With the help of Edith's husband Valentine Blakemoor, Lucy had leased a property that was ideally situated for their manufacturing business. Her company, Chartrand's Toilette Preparations, had blossomed. As had her family.

"Brava, darling," Gareth told her. "Say brava, Fan-Fan."

Fanny clapped again, her dark ringlets bouncing in her enthusiasm. "Bwava! Bwava, Mama!"

"Hercules, speak," Gareth commanded.

And the pug's head tilted to the side before he emitted a delighted bark.

Lucy chuckled, closing the distance between herself and her little family. "Thank you, my loves." She gave Hercules a loving scratch on the head before wrapping her arms around her husband and daughter. "I'm the luckiest woman in all London."

She dropped a kiss on her daughter's soft cheek and then another on her husband's, the prickle of his stubble an abrasion on her lips that was every bit as welcome as the scent of her newly formulated after-shaving balm on his skin.

"I have a feeling luck didn't have a thing to do with it," Gareth said, smiling down at her, handsome and utterly at ease. "I'm so proud of you, Lucy. You've worked hard to build your cosmetics business. I'm going to buy the entire stock of Chartrand's cream from Bellingham and Co. the moment it's on sale."

She smiled at his devotion. "Thank you, my love. But you ought to leave some for the customers."

"I'll leave two," he promised.

She kissed him on the lips, not caring if the servants saw.

Fanny clapped, interrupting the moment with a delighted, "Mama! Papa!"

Lucy and Gareth laughed, ending the kiss before it could truly begin.

"We have an audience, Mama," her husband reminded her.

"How could I forget that the youngest member of the Lady's Suffrage Society is always watching?" she teased, ruffling Fanny's glossy curls.

"Always," Gareth said, smiling back at her, so much love and joy shining in his eyes that she had to blink away the tears rising in hers. "I wouldn't have it any other way, darling."

"Nor would I," she said.

∽

GARETH NEARLY SWALLOWED his tongue when he saw his wife that evening in their bedroom. Not her room—that had been transformed into a sitting room and bathroom, complete with the most modern of features—electric lighting and hot water to fill the oversized tub they often shared, bathing each other until their tender ministrations turned into something more.

But *their* room.

The one that had once been his.

The place he had hidden himself away from her in the earliest weeks of their marriage, denying his heart and body what they both so desperately wanted. He didn't give a damn if it wasn't done, if a husband and wife sharing a room was *de trop* in polite society. Didn't care if the servants wagged their tongues and spread gossip about them all across London.

He loved having her here with him. Loved spending each night with her in bed. Loved *her*. He fell asleep to the deep, even sound of her breathing, for she always succumbed to slumber first. And it soothed him. The nightmares that had once plagued him, the very ones that had led him to the midnight gardens the night they had first kissed, had long since been banished.

"Do you like it?" she asked mischievously, fingering the nearly transparent night rail she wore that was fashioned of pure silk.

Beneath it, her breasts were ripe and succulent, her nipples hard and erect, begging to be sucked. The faintest, most tantalizing hint of pink he'd ever beheld beckoned to him from the other side of that decadent fabric, along with the shadow between her legs.

"I'm not certain if I like it more on you or off you," he confessed, stalking toward her.

"Perhaps I should leave it on for the night," she teased.

"Take it off," he said instantly, before remembering he aspired to be a gentleman and adding, "please."

"I saw it at Bellingham and Co.," she told him with a wicked smile. "I thought of you."

"As if I needed further reason to find you utterly delectable," he growled, sliding an arm around her waist and pulling her into his frame so she could feel the effect she had on him. His cock was painfully hard, desperate to be inside her.

But then, that seemed to be a perpetual state. Love and happiness had that effect upon a man. And he was damned fortunate to know it.

"It certainly seems as if you approve," she murmured wickedly, her hand slipping between them to find his rigid length, cupping and stroking him through the thin layer of his own dressing gown.

"I approve more than you know." He lowered his head and took her lips in a kiss that quickly deepened.

He fed her his tongue and she moaned, sucking on it while she continued to play with his erection. His hips pumped into her expert touch mindlessly, chasing, needing. And God, it was good, so good. He trusted himself completely with this woman. Trusted her implicitly. They knew each other's secrets, bodies, desires, hopes. Slowly, meticulously, she had freed him of the shackles of his past. One by one, until nothing had remained.

She caught his lower lip in her teeth, delivering a playful nip, and he groaned, knowing he would never tire of the way she embraced her sensual nature. She was perfect for him in every way. Everything he wanted, all he needed.

He ended the kiss, his breathing ragged, to catch a handful of silk warmed by her skin in his grasp, giving it a tug. "Off, Lady Rexingham."

"As my lord wishes," she told him with a minx's smile, and then she relinquished her hold on his cock to grasp twin fists of silk and haul the night rail over her head. It sailed through the air and landed on the Axminster behind her with a soft whoosh of sound.

She was naked.

Naked and beautiful.

A fierce sense of possession shot through Gareth, searing him. He took her sweet lips with his, kissing her, holding her, and guided her backward, leading her to their bed. When the backs of her knees finally hit the edge of the mattress, he paused, helping her to climb into the high tester before joining her.

She looked perfect. She looked like *his* lying there, all cream and pink loveliness, so feminine and curved and tempting.

"I want to lick you," he told her, overwhelmed with desire.

Not bothering with anything fanciful or practiced. Just pure, unadulterated need.

"Yes," she murmured, lying on her back, reclining amongst the many pillows and spreading her legs in invitation.

He didn't need further prodding.

Gareth joined her on the bed, kissing and caressing up her soft, well-curved legs and along her inner thighs, savoring each patch of silken skin, every soft sigh that emitted from her lush, pink lips. He splayed his hands, nudging her legs farther apart. Glistening folds beckoned, and he dipped his head, helpless to do anything but spoil her with his mouth, his tongue. He sucked her bud, then licked up and down her seam until he found her entrance, teasing her with short parries until he finally plunged deep. The taste of her was decadent and musky.

He lapped at her, reveling in her husky sounds of desire, the way her fingers sifted through his hair, grasping handfuls and tugging when he applied greater pressure. He wanted her undone. Wanted her to lose control. To reach her pinnacle from nothing more than his lips and tongue and teeth. And she was gratifyingly close, so close, already hovering on that tender precipice.

A little nibble, a lick followed by a suck. And then again, again, again until she was coming, gasping beneath him, her hips undulating, seeking, needing. He stayed with her, laving her pearl, licking up and down her slit, filling her again with his tongue as she moaned and shuddered, caught helplessly in the grip of her own restless desire.

Finally, when he couldn't withstand another moment of sensual torture, of waiting, of not being deep inside her where he most longed to be, he tore his mouth from her cunny, leveraging his larger body over hers. He braced himself on his forearms, grasping his painfully ready cock, dragging it over her drenched folds to coat himself in her dew.

"I love you," he told her, and then he pushed forward, sliding inside her wet heat.

She surrounded him, pulling him deeper, and he found the tip of one perfect breast, sucking hard as she gasped and writhed, driving him on with breathy pants and low moans of pleasure.

"I love you so much," she gasped as he thrust again, harder this time, to the hilt, their hip bones pressed intimately against each other, her nipple hard and greedy in his mouth as he suckled.

He found a rhythm that had them both on the edge, pumping in and out of her until they were gasping for breath. But he wanted more. Deeper. He withdrew entirely and then turned her onto her stomach, positioning her on her knees with her bottom in the air, and then he slid into her again, the angle impossibly good. So good that he almost came instantly.

Gritting his teeth, he struggled to temper his desire, to last. But she felt wonderful, tightening on him, and he knew he was going to come too quickly. She was slick, hot, and... damn it.

"God, Lucy, you feel so wonderful."

"I'm going to come," she told him, a needy tone in her voice that only made him more desperate to lose himself inside her. "Make me come."

Her wanton demand had its intended effect on him.

Gareth fucked her harder, his fingers tightening on her hips as he worked himself in and out of her drenched sheath, watching his cock, glistening with her juices, glide in and out, in and out. Faster now. He slammed into her with a punishing rhythm, then reached for her pearl with his right hand, rubbing it until she gasped and bucked, and a torrent of liquid bathed his cock as she spent all over him.

"Yes," she gasped out, grasping the bedsheets with white knuckles. "Fill me. Fuck me."

She knew he had a particular weakness for her saying filthy things to him, and this time was no different. As she rode out her climax, he redoubled his efforts, using short, quick strokes to find what he needed. Ecstasy exploded from the base of his spine, his ballocks contracting as he spilled inside her, filling her with his seed until he was spent and collapsed against her back, breathing hard, his cock still buried deep inside her.

"Again," she pleaded, wiggling her hips and bringing his deflating prick back to attention.

"Jesus," he muttered. "You'll kill me, woman."

"I hope not," she murmured, glancing at him over her bare shoulder, her mahogany hair a wild tangle around her face. "Our children need their father."

His heart was pounding so loudly from the force of his release that he was sure he'd misheard her. "We've only the one," he pointed out, withdrawing and rolling to his back at her side, sated and utterly spent.

"For the moment," Lucy said with a secretive air.

His head jerked toward hers. "Lucy? Are you?"

She smiled, the happiness wreathing her face making her even more beautiful than she already was. "Pregnant? Yes. I am. It's early, but our family is about to grow again."

"And I've just…damn it," he cursed, raking a hand through his hair. "I didn't hurt you, did I? Did I take you too roughly? I should have taken more care—"

"Hush," she interrupted, pressing a finger over his lips. "Not another word. You ought to know by now that I'm an American, and we're as healthy as horses. Everything you did was perfect." She removed her finger and kissed him soundly before lifting her head and meeting his gaze. "And I expect you to do it again in approximately fifteen minutes."

Gareth bit out a laugh. "Ah, my American firebrand, what would I do without you?"

"You'd be lost," she said fondly.

"Yes," he agreed, pulling her against his side where she belonged. "I would."

"It's a good thing I mistook you for the footman that night," his minx of a wife added tartly. "You may thank me later."

"Don't remind me about the damned footman," he growled. "Reginald can go to the devil. You're mine, and I'm keeping you."

The bastard's name had been Robert. Gareth would never forget it. But he also took great delight in calling him by the wrong name.

"I am indeed yours," Lucy said, looking at him in a way that made him feel omnipotent, as if he were the only man in the world. "Whatever will you do with me?"

A challenge if he'd ever heard one.

"I'll show you, my love," he promised.

And he did.

THANK you for reading Lucy and Gareth's happily ever after! I hope you adored their love story as much as I enjoyed writing it. A few little notes before you move on to the sneak peek of Charity and Viscount Wilton's new and improved happily ever after in *Forever Her Viscount*... Lucy's cosmetics business was inspired by real-life entrepreneur Harriet Hubbard Ayer. Lark Square is a product of my imagination, but otherwise, I strove to accurately depict Victorian London, including the walk to Hyde Park and the visit to the opera. I'm indebted to my late 19th century travel guide for all such important details. The department store Bellingham and Co. is a product of my imagination loosely based on Harding, Howell & Co., largely considered to be the first department store in England. You may recall its original appearance in *Sutton's Scandal*; naturally, Lily and Tarquin's offspring have kept his department store thriving! And if you're wondering who Madeline married, keep an eye out for book 6. I intentionally omitted details in this book to avoid spoilers.

Please stay in touch! The only way to be sure you'll know what's next from me is to sign up for my newsletter here: http://eepurl.com/dyJSar. Please join my reader group for early excerpts, cover reveals, and more here: https://www.facebook.com/groups/scarlettscottreaders. And if you're in the mood to chat all things steamy historical romance and read a different book together each month, join my book club, Dukes Do It Hotter right here: https://www.facebook.com/groups/hotdukes because we're having a whole lot of fun! Now, on to that sneak peek of Charity and Wilton's story...

Forever Her Viscount

After a salacious rumor tarnished her reputation and caused the man she loved to cry off their engagement, Lady Charity Manners has dedicated herself to becoming an unapologetic hoyden. She'll never fall in love with a man—or trust one—ever again. Especially not a quiet, brooding, proper lord who is too handsome for his own good.

Neville Astley, Viscount Wilton, is a recluse by choice who has mostly avoided society until becoming the guardian of his niece. For her sake, he's attending a Yorkshire country house party, despite preferring to be anywhere else. He wants nothing to do with romance or a wild hellion like Lady Charity. And yet, there's something about her that he finds impossible to resist.

Unexpected desire flares between the gentleman most likely to follow the rules and the lady most likely to break them. But while Charity will surrender her body willingly, she'll never cede her heart. When Neville realizes he wants far more from her than a midnight tryst, he'll do everything he can to persuade her that the only place she belongs is in his arms—forever.

Chapter One

Neville Astley, Fifteenth Viscount Wilton, hated most people.

While he abhorred social gatherings of every sort, no abomination was quite as hideously wretched to endure as the country house party. To him, country house parties were the equivalent of walking barefoot through the wilds of Scotland in the coldest depths of winter. He'd rather subject himself to any other form of torture. But for his older brother's only daughter, he would do anything, even if it meant playing life-sized lawn chess in Yorkshire or being chased by an irate swan. Even if it meant listening to dreadful singing and playing companion to a potted palm during a ball.

Even if it meant inadvertently catching Lady Charity Manners swimming in nothing but her chemise during his customary early-morning walk.

He hadn't intended to linger when he first heard the rhythmic sound of water splashing. Nor when he'd discovered the tidy heap of feminine garments that suggested whoever was swimming was not just a lady, but also one who was wearing shockingly little.

She wasn't completely naked as she emerged from the

sparkling Sherborne Manor lake just now, the chemise plastered lovingly over the contours of her well-curved form. But she may as well have been. Before him stood the most compelling evidence that the rumor about the scandalous nude Venus painting was true. Because she looked every bit as glorious and beautiful as the picture he'd seen on display at the Grosvenor Gallery.

She had posed for it.

He was certain.

The knowledge was astonishing. He couldn't fathom the daring she must possess. Not just to sit naked for the painting's lurid depiction of the goddess, but to swim at a house party, wearing a garment that was essentially transparent.

Neville was horrified. He was also—and quite against his better judgment—moved. Every part of her was perfectly formed, a temptation he couldn't seem to stop devouring with his gaze, even though the gentleman in him knew he ought to look away.

"Lord Wilton," she said brightly, as if they had met under ordinary circumstances and he couldn't see her nipples through that wet scrap of linen. "You're taking your morning walk early today."

He was, by half an hour.

How the devil did she know? More importantly, why was she not making any move to cover herself?

"You ought to dress, Lady Charity," he said stiffly. "For the sake of your modesty."

Where was her chaperone? She had come to the house party with her aunt. The woman clearly had no notion what manner of mischief her charge was making. Either way, she was fortunate that it was Neville who had happened upon her and not one of the other guests.

She shrugged carelessly as she wrung water from her hair. "Haven't you heard? I don't have any modesty."

Of course he had heard. Everyone in England had heard. But he'd never bothered to mire himself in speculation and gossip. Nor had he given much thought to a woman he'd never supposed he would meet.

"Perhaps you should have some," he countered in the same stern voice he used for his beloved niece whenever she was wayward.

Which, unfortunately for Neville, was frequently.

In the wake of his older brother and sister-in-law's deaths over a year ago, Neville had become Margaret's guardian. To say he had been unprepared for the gravity of his role would have been a vast understatement. Margaret made trouble wherever she went. He had no notion of what to do with a twenty-year-old with a penchant for waywardness. His current plan was to do everything he could to keep her from eloping with a scoundrel, or being compromised by one.

"Modesty is dreadfully boring, I'm afraid," Lady Charity told him breezily, still squeezing water from her golden plait. "I'd rather be able to splash about in the lake whenever I choose. It's so much more fun."

"Fun," he repeated.

"An amusement," she said, a teasing grin on her lips. "A diversion."

"I'm aware of the word's definition," he bit out, trying not to stare at the round fullness of her breasts straining against her chemise and failing utterly.

He should go. Leave her here to dress. Pretend it had never happened. That he'd never seen the pink points of her hard nipples poking through her chemise like a taunt for his mouth. And yet, his feet refused to cooperate. He remained, as if he were one of the nearby trees and had grown roots.

"You seemed unfamiliar with it." Her smile grew. "I thought perhaps I could enlighten you."

She was teasing him. Not just teasing. *Flirting.* She

released her braid and her hands moved to her chemise, grasping the wet fabric.

Surely she didn't intend to remove it.

His neck went hot. "Stop at once, madam."

She didn't. The hem of her chemise lifted, revealing her calves, then her knees. By God. She was going to remove it entirely. He didn't want her to do so. And yet, he also very badly did.

But then she paused, gathering the skirt of her undergarment, twisting it, and wringing it out the same way she had her hair.

He could breathe again, but his cock was hard and insistent in his trousers. Inconvenient desire burned through him. Desire he had no business feeling for the maddening Lady Charity Manners.

"What did you think I was going to do?" she asked him with a conspiratorial air. "Take it off?"

Yes, he had. Because he was having thoughts he distinctly should not be having for this outrageous hoyden. He had to think of Margaret, for heaven's sake. Her reputation would suffer should he cause any sort of scandal.

And after losing both her parents, Margaret deserved happiness. She deserved a fine husband, one she'd never find if Neville surrendered to his base instincts and kissed a nearly nude Lady Charity Manners. Because he wouldn't want to stop at kissing.

More warmth crawled up his neck, his ears going hot.

"What part of England has the most dogs?" he blurted.

Oh, lovely. Apparently, he was reverting to his habit of telling dreadful jokes whenever the nervousness that inevitably seized him returned.

Lady Charity's brow furrowed. "I have no notion why you've just asked me that, my lord."

She continued wringing out her chemise, pulling it a bit

higher and revealing a swath of thigh that would haunt him in his dreams tonight.

"To distract myself," he muttered.

"From what?"

"From your unfortunate state of *dishabille*, Lady Charity," Neville clarified rigidly.

"Oh." Her full lips curved into a sensual smile. "I suppose I've shocked you, but how else was I meant to swim? A lady could drown, bogged down by so many layers. And wouldn't it be positively horrid for me to be unmannerly enough to perish at the Duke and Duchess of Bradford's country house party? So you see, wearing only my chemise for my dip in the lake was actually quite practical of me."

He didn't see anything practical about her transparent chemise or the shadow between her thighs or the way her undergarment clung to her, lovingly revealing her lush figure.

"Bark-shire," he answered for her instead of responding to her ridiculous claim. "Instead of *Berkshire*. The part of England with the most dogs, that is."

Lady Charity stared at him.

"It's a pun," he added faintly.

"I'm aware," she said dryly, echoing his words earlier.

He winced. This was why he loathed Society. Why he had always eschewed large gatherings until Margaret's period of mourning had ended and he'd been forced to reemerge from his haven in the countryside. Why he dreaded every moment he had to spend in polite conversation. Because he was horrible at it. His brother, Wentworth, had been the garrulous and silver-tongued charmer. He'd been at his best when surrounded by others. Neville, meanwhile, had been content to keep to himself. To keep from humiliating himself just as he was doing now before this stunning, brazen woman.

"You ought to dress before someone else comes along on the path," he forced out. "You'll cause a scandal."

She laughed, the sound mellifluous. "No one would be surprised if the disgraceful Lady Charity Manners caused another scandal. Surely, my reputation proceeds me."

Was there a hint of bitterness in her voice? Neville thought so.

As if she had all the time in the world to dress, she reached for a petticoat lying atop the pile.

"I don't indulge in frivolous gossip," he told her politely rather than admit that he was indeed aware of the rumors concerning her.

Perhaps worse, that he believed them.

She gave him a searching look, shaking out her petticoat. "Since you're here, you may as well help me."

Help her? That would require proximity.

His denial was swift. "It would be unseemly."

A soft chuckle fell from her lips. "More unseemly than standing here conversing while I'm in my shift? I think not. Come closer, won't you? My bodice has a rather frustrating line of buttons on the back, and I had to twist and contort myself to open them."

She made everything sound practical. As if it were a matter of course that he help her dress. As if it were perfectly ordinary for an unwed lady—or any lady, for that matter—to go about swimming in a lake, nearly nude. What a peculiar woman she was. He found himself annoyingly intrigued.

And moving closer. Damn it, what was this effect she had on him?

Want more? Get *Forever Her Viscount* now!

DON'T MISS SCARLETT'S OTHER ROMANCES!

Complete Book List
HISTORICAL ROMANCE

Heart's Temptation
A Mad Passion (Book One)
Rebel Love (Book Two)
Reckless Need (Book Three)
Sweet Scandal (Book Four)
Restless Rake (Book Five)
Darling Duke (Book Six)
The Night Before Scandal (Book Seven)

Wicked Husbands
Her Errant Earl (Book One)
Her Lovestruck Lord (Book Two)
Her Reformed Rake (Book Three)
Her Deceptive Duke (Book Four)
Her Missing Marquess (Book Five)
Her Virtuous Viscount (Book Six)

League of Dukes
Nobody's Duke (Book One)
Heartless Duke (Book Two)
Dangerous Duke (Book Three)
Shameless Duke (Book Four)
Scandalous Duke (Book Five)
Fearless Duke (Book Six)

Notorious Ladies of London
Lady Ruthless (Book One)
Lady Wallflower (Book Two)
Lady Reckless (Book Three)
Lady Wicked (Book Four)
Lady Lawless (Book Five)
Lady Brazen (Book 6)

Unexpected Lords
The Detective Duke (Book One)
The Playboy Peer (Book Two)
The Millionaire Marquess (Book Three)
The Goodbye Governess (Book Four)

Dukes Most Wanted
Forever Her Duke (Book One)
Forever Her Marquess (Book Two)
Forever Her Rake (Book Three)
Forever Her Earl (Book Four)
Forever Her Viscount (Book Five)

The Wicked Winters
Wicked in Winter (Book One)
Wedded in Winter (Book Two)
Wanton in Winter (Book Three)
Wishes in Winter (Book 3.5)

Willful in Winter (Book Four)
Wagered in Winter (Book Five)
Wild in Winter (Book Six)
Wooed in Winter (Book Seven)
Winter's Wallflower (Book Eight)
Winter's Woman (Book Nine)
Winter's Whispers (Book Ten)
Winter's Waltz (Book Eleven)
Winter's Widow (Book Twelve)
Winter's Warrior (Book Thirteen)
A Merry Wicked Winter (Book Fourteen)

The Sinful Suttons
Sutton's Spinster (Book One)
Sutton's Sins (Book Two)
Sutton's Surrender (Book Three)
Sutton's Seduction (Book Four)
Sutton's Scoundrel (Book Five)
Sutton's Scandal (Book Six)
Sutton's Secrets (Book Seven)

Rogue's Guild
Her Ruthless Duke (Book One)
Her Dangerous Beast (Book Two)
Her Wicked Rogue (Book 3)

Royals and Renegades
How to Love a Dangerous Rogue (Book One)

Sins and Scoundrels
Duke of Depravity
Prince of Persuasion
Marquess of Mayhem
Sarah

Earl of Every Sin
Duke of Debauchery
Viscount of Villainy

Sins and Scoundrels Box Set Collections
Volume 1
Volume 2

The Wicked Winters Box Set Collections
Collection 1
Collection 2
Collection 3
Collection 4

Wicked Husbands Box Set Collections
Volume 1
Volume 2

Stand-alone Novella
Lord of Pirates

CONTEMPORARY ROMANCE
Love's Second Chance
Reprieve (Book One)
Perfect Persuasion (Book Two)
Win My Love (Book Three)

Coastal Heat
Loved Up (Book One)

ABOUT THE AUTHOR

USA Today and Amazon bestselling author Scarlett Scott writes steamy Victorian and Regency romance with strong, intelligent heroines and sexy alpha heroes. She lives in Pennsylvania and Maryland with her Canadian husband, their adorable identical twins, two sweet dogs, and one zany cat.

A self-professed literary junkie and nerd, she loves reading anything, but especially romance novels, poetry, and Middle English verse. Catch up with her on her website https://scarlettscottauthor.com. Hearing from readers never fails to make her day.

Scarlett's complete book list and information about upcoming releases can be found at https://scarlettscottauthor.com.

Connect with Scarlett! You can find her here:
    Join Scarlett Scott's reader group on Facebook for early excerpts, giveaways, and a whole lot of fun!
    Sign up for her newsletter here
    https://www.tiktok.com/@authorscarlettscott

facebook.com/AuthorScarlettScott

x.com/scarscoromance

instagram.com/scarlettscottauthor

bookbub.com/authors/scarlett-scott

amazon.com/Scarlett-Scott/e/B004NW8N2I

pinterest.com/scarlettscott

Made in the USA
Las Vegas, NV
02 November 2024

10951213R00121